Dear Sly,

I know what you're thinking. I get to Australia, I meet a man, I get married. Just like that. Foolish, impulsive Rusty. Well, it's not what it looks like. Daniel Marlin is a hulking Aussie cowboy, a down under Romeo who thinks he's God's gift to the universe. It's just that Daniel's job as a tour guide suddenly depended on his being married, and I was the only believable choice. And he and my cousin Alan are saving to start their own business, and I adore Alan. Anyway, that's how it is. So I'm staying in Oz a little longer. I'll be in the middle of the outback if you need me, on tour with my "husband." Did I mention I'll be cooking for everyone over a campfire? And sleeping in Daniel's tent? Good thing he's so obnoxious. Otherwise, who knows what might happen on one of those starry outback nights?

Lovingly,

Rusty

P.S. Please send me a cookbook. Express.

Please address questions and book requests to: Silhouette Reader Service
U.S.: 3010 Walden Ave., P.O. Box 1325, Buffalo, NY 14269
Canadian: P.O. Box 609, Fort Erie, Ont. L2A 5X3

Make-Believe Matrimony

EMILIE RICHARDS
OUTBACK NIGHTS

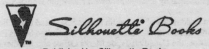

Silhouette Books

Published by Silhouette Books

America's Publisher of Contemporary Romance

SILHOUETTE BOOKS
300 East 42nd St.,
New York, N.Y. 10017

ISBN 0-373-30129-4

OUTBACK NIGHTS

Copyright © 1987 by Emilie Richards McGee

Celebrity Wedding Certificates published by permission of
Donald Ray Pounders from *Celebrity Wedding Ceremonies*.

Printed in U.S.A.

A Letter from the Author

Dear Reader,

Ten years ago my husband and I packed up our four children and traveled to Australia, where we lived and worked for five glorious months. The trip was our first out of the United States, and everything we did was wonderfully new. To this day our children still talk about the friends they made and the sights they saw. The trip brought us closer as a family and gave us memories we'll never forget. So when we were offered the chance to go again later this year, we grabbed it without hesitation. In just three short months of my writing this letter, my husband, youngest son and I will get on a plane and fly to Adelaide once more.

Australia is a magical place. I've set four books there, all in places that I visited. *Outback Nights* is certainly one of my favorites, since I took the actual trip that Daniel and Rusty take in this book, camping and exploring Australia's fascinating interior. I suspect there will be more Australia books in my future, since on this trip we plan to travel to parts of the country that we didn't see before. I have an idea for a book about... But I guess I shouldn't give anything away.

I'm pleased that Silhouette is re-releasing *Outback Nights,* and I hope you enjoy your outback trek as much as I enjoyed mine. Settle in with Rusty as she learns some of what marriage is all about. And fall in love with Daniel, if you dare. Fall in love with Australia, too. I know I did.

Emilie Richards

For the crew and passengers
of the Northern Queen,
especially Maureen, Phil and Jill.
Next time, Birdsville.

Prologue

"If you'll move a little to the left, I can make a clean dive out that window." Sly Jackson pointed one short, well-manicured finger at the far side of the room.

Russet Ames focused unblinking amber eyes on the man in front of her. She didn't move an inch. "Go ahead, Sly. I was expecting a guilt trip. Make it a good one."

"Why didn't you just pull a gun and shoot me? You could have ended it all with one quick blast so I wouldn't suffer like this!"

Russet's mouth turned up at the corners. "I believe it's illegal to shoot people. Even in Manhattan."

"You'd have been acquitted. It would have been a mercy killing."

"You're going to recover."

Sly shook his head forlornly and wrenched open the giant jar of antacid tablets he kept on his desk as a monument to the stress he experienced daily. It was the first time in the four years Russet had known him that she'd actually seen him open the jar. She wondered how old the tablets were.

"Why'd you do it?" He crunched noisily between words in emphasis. "Why the hell did you do it?"

"I thought you'd never ask."

He waved aside her answer. "It doesn't even matter. The point is that yesterday you were a salable commodity. Aura was going to offer you big bucks to renew your contract. The sky was the limit."

"I know all that." Russet walked to the window and gazed out at the city she loved. Sly's office was in a building so old that whatever period it represented had been long since forgotten in the annals of architectural history. But the view from his window was unmistakably contemporary New York City. Russet loved the view. She loved the city. She felt a twinge of regret for decisions made.

"You must like to suffer. You must like to see me suffer."

"All this because I cut my hair." Russet raised her hands to the mass of short, boyish curls covering her head. "It's just hair, Sly. Strings of dead cells. There was no pain involved, no suffering. You're my agent, not my conscience."

"Just hair? That hair was worth thousands; millions maybe. That was some of the best-known hair in the United States. At this moment there are probably a thousand little teenyboppers in this country alone trying to find hair that color in a bottle so they'll look like Russet Ames, the Aura Girl."

Russet shuddered. "What an awful thought."

"Why'd you do it?"

Russet didn't remind him that he'd said it didn't matter why. "Sly, how would you like it if one thing about you became so important that nothing else mattered?"

"I don't know what you're talking about."

Russet turned back to him. "Let's say your nose became famous—" she smiled mischievously "—or your pot belly. When people looked at you, they saw only that part of you. Other middle-aged men started gaining weight to imitate you; you had to stand for hours while people took pictures of your belly."

"Cut the comedy, Russet." Sly grabbed another handful of tablets.

"I'll make it simple, then: I want to be me."

"Somebody put those words to music and made a fortune. You just lost a fortune. And so did I," he added heavily. "I owned ten percent of that hair."

"It's probably still on the floor of Mimi's Hairway to Heaven. You could go collect your cut." She laughed at his disgusted glare. "Sorry, no pun intended."

"You know you're finished. No one's going to want you anymore."

"That was the whole point." Russet shook her head, marveling anew at its lightness now that it was minus a good two feet of hair. How could she explain the impulse that had made her walk through the door of the second-rate beauty salon to put an end to her modeling career? How could she explain her fatigue, her restlessness, her growing sense of the absurdity of her life? No matter what she said, she knew that Sly, who measured all things by their price, would not understand. She tried anyway. "I never wanted to be a model. You know that. This whole Aura thing just steamrolled me."

"I never heard you complain when the checks came in."

"I'm grateful for the experience and for the money." She walked around the desk and stood on tiptoe to kiss his cheek. "And I'm grateful for all you've done. But I'm off on new adventures now."

Sly's anger and curiosity warred openly across his features. Then he sighed, and Russet knew the battle had been won. At least temporarily. "What are you going to do?" he asked, resignation heavy in his voice.

"I'm going to Australia."

"I should have known. Couldn't you have run any farther? Wasn't the South Pole open for tourists?"

"Did you know my mother was from Australia? I've never been there; she hasn't been back herself since she married my father. But I've got a cousin there. I want to meet him and explore the country."

"They probably don't even sell Aura shampoo in Australia."

"They don't. I checked before I bought my ticket."

Sly was silent for a minute. Then he began to speak slowly, gaining momentum as he went. "It's possible, there's one chance in a million, that Aura might like this new look. There's nothing glamorous about you now; you look like a healthy little girl. But that might be good. All those fitness nuts and sports fanatics might be impressed by the new you. We could photograph you in a leotard or a tennis dress."

"I'll send you a boomerang." Russet patted Sly's cheek and then began to back away. "I'll write every day once I get there."

"We could get some shots of you in a health club working on some of those machines, maybe with a headband."

Russet reached the door. "Goodbye, Sly. Take care of yourself." She pulled the door toward her and disappeared into the reception area.

"Or maybe," he continued, "maybe they'd like you in a swimsuit. One of those French-cut numbers. Sleek and black..." He stopped, visualizing Russet's curvaceous body in just such a garment. "You could come out of the pool and shampoo your hair,'' he muttered to himself. "Aura is mild enough to use every day, it strips away harmful chemicals as it cleans and conditions. Annie,'' he yelled through the open door, "get Henry Biddler at Aura on the telephone. Tell him it's urgent.''

Chapter One

Dear Sly,

Nice try, old buddy, but I meant what I said. If Henry is still waiting for me to show up for that appointment, he's going to have to wait a long time. My plane is over South Australia circling Adelaide at this very moment.

Has it ever occurred to you that we worked so well together because we're both impulsive, stubborn, and always certain we're right? Run that one by your analyst!

Anyway, Sly dear, since leaving New York, not one person has looked twice at me. I'm Rusty now, not Russet, and the clothes I brought with me carry only the Union label. I went to a tanning salon and got a beautiful crop of freckles, and I haven't used Aura shampoo in a week.

You know what else? I've never felt happier!

Notice there's no address on this letter? I'll bet you can guess why. Good luck in finding a new Aura girl.

Sympathetically,
Rusty

She had escaped!

Rusty scrawled Sly's address across the front of an envelope and stuffed in the letter. It would probably take two weeks to reach him. In that time his indigestion would have stabilized and his search to find a new client to replace her would have begun. Sly had an eye for finding the right girl for the right product. When Henry Biddler got over his fury at losing Russet Ames, he would turn to Sly to get him a replacement. Rusty felt no guilt over her decision. Sly would survive this just fine.

But if she felt no guilt, she certainly had other feelings. As the plane began its descent over the velvet-green Adelaide Hills, she was a seething cauldron of emotions. Excitement ranked first, followed by pure sentimentality. Mixed in with these were small doses of nostalgia for what she'd left and apprehension for what was to come. Throw it all together with a bad case of jet lag and the new sensation of being just one in a crowd, and the result was her present state of mind.

Maybe it was just exhaustion brought on by a twenty-four-hour journey, or maybe it was the same peculiar urge that had brought her to Australia in the first place, but Rusty had to grip the arms of her seat to force herself to remain in place as the plane landed. She wanted to be the first one out the door. She wanted to forget etiquette and the fact she was an ambassador for her country and push past all the people in front of her. She wanted to be surrounded by the warmth of sunshine instead of the warmth of human bodies.

Instead, she schooled herself to sit quietly and tap her foot until it was time to stand and file in an orderly fashion down the aisle. The airplane doors would open soon, and she would be set free. There would be no customs lines to go through here in Adelaide; she'd already been through them in Sydney. Once she was off the plane, her new life would begin. She had only to collect her suitcases and find Alan.

Cousin Alan—Rusty smiled wearily at the thought. Having a real, live cousin would take some getting used to. It was just one thing of many that would seem strange here. But she was looking forward to getting to know Alan and his wife Penny even more than she was looking forward to seeing kangaroos and koalas.

"Someone meeting you?"

Rusty turned to the old man who had been her seatmate on the flight from Sydney. "My cousin's coming. I've never seen him, but he said he'd be wearing a T-shirt with Outback Odysseys printed on it."

The man winked. "Best tour company in South Australia, but there's a mob of larrikins in that outfit. Hope he's not one of them."

Rusty was still trying to figure out what a larrikin was when everyone stood and began to move toward the airplane door. Whatever a larrikin was, she doubted that Alan Benedict qualified. She'd been corresponding with him since childhood. His letters were models of penmanship and perfect English. He'd married at age twenty-two, become a father at twenty-three and was about to become a father again at twenty-five. His wife, Penny, was a former schoolteacher who often added notes to Alan's letters. Sight unseen, Rusty loved them both.

At the bottom of the airplane steps, she forcibly disciplined herself not to kneel and kiss the runway. Ground, sweet ground! It was home, sweet home—even if she'd never been here before. She was part Australian, if such a designation could apply to a nation as young as this one, and the land down under had called to her since she'd first learned of her connection to it.

The October sun shone brightly on the cherry-colored curls that faithfully honored the name given to her before she'd had any hair at all. It had been autumn in New York when she'd left. Brief stops in Honolulu and Sydney had helped prepare her for a switch to spring, but now, with the Australian sun warming her skin and setting fire to her hair, she felt for the first time how far she'd come: far enough to have come through the looking glass. For a moment she almost felt she was walking upside down.

Inside the terminal she stood, scanning the crowd for her cousin. Through her fatigue, or maybe because of it, she could feel her excitement build, threatening to carry her away on its tide.

Alan had described himself as ordinary, and the only picture she had of him as an adult had been sufficiently overexposed and out of focus not to disprove him. Now Rusty searched for a healthy-looking, bearded young man wearing an orange and blue T-shirt like the one Alan had once sent her as a Christmas present. She might not recognize Alan, but there would be no chance of missing the neon colors of the T-shirt or the logo of a smirking kangaroo with two tourists clinging to its back while another tourist with binoculars peeked out of its pouch.

The airport crowd had cleared considerably before Rusty glimpsed the orange and blue signal. Apparently Alan had been late arriving because now he strode in from the direction of the parking lot, his hands in the pockets of tight jeans. He had the look of a man with a mission.

Even from a distance she could see that neither Alan's picture nor his description had done him justice. She was filled with a surge of familial pride. This man, sturdy and handsome and in his prime, was related to her. He was probably just six foot although he was still inches taller than she was, but he moved with a certain swagger that said everything about the way he viewed himself. His shoulders were broad and his waistline trim. His hair under a wide-brimmed felt hat was brown and a little too long, as if he couldn't be bothered to get a haircut. The beard of the picture was gone, revealing a square, firm chin that said everything about his temperament. As he came closer she registered the bluest eyes she'd ever seen and a smile that flashed white fire against richly tanned skin.

In a moment she'd thrown herself into his arms in a burst of sentimental enthusiasm.

"Alan." Rusty flung her arms around her cousin's neck. "Alan!"

"I—"

"I'm so glad to be here!" Rusty stood on tiptoe and kissed his cheek. "You have no idea how glad."

"I'm glad you're here, too, only I'm..."

Rusty was too excited to listen to his words. She stepped back a little to get a better view. "And you said you were just ordinary. Ordinary? You're gorgeous! Are all Australian men that modest? I should have asked Penny for a description of you. I'm sure she'd have told me the truth. If it hadn't been for the T-shirt..."

Alan took off his hat, running his fingers through his hair. "About the T-shirt—"

"Don't apologize. I wouldn't have been able to spot you without it, and besides, it's perfect on you. It sets off that fantastic tan—and those eyes! You must have gotten those eyes from your father. Nobody on my side of the family has eyes like that."

The eyes in question began to sparkle. "Well, I..."

Rusty framed Alan's face in her hands. "All those years I wanted to meet you. And here you are. In the flesh."

Alan flashed a brilliant smile, and his arms locked behind her waist. "The flesh," he repeated softly, even as she interrupted him yet again.

"My cousin," she said fondly.

He pulled her closer. "I didn't expect such a bang-up greeting."

"We Yanks can get pretty exuberant," she teased him. "It's just that I've wanted to meet you for so long." She clasped her hands behind his neck and rose to kiss his cheek again.

"We Aussies can get right exuberant, too." Alan pulled her closer. "Right exuberant. Welcome to Oz."

It was only when Alan's arms tightened around her waist and his mouth replaced the smooth feel of his cheek against her lips that Rusty began to wonder about Australian customs and kissing cousins.

Alan's kiss was thorough and practiced and decidedly uncousinly. He quite simply took her apart and put her back together again at his leisure. And Rusty, who was caught completely off guard, had no idea how to respond.

"Alan..." She tried to squirm away from him when it seemed he was finished.

"So glad you're here," he said, pulling her back and kissing her again.

She got a glimpse of deep lines of laughter etched in his dark tan before she was caught up in another kiss. Whatever else was going on, Alan was certainly enjoying this moment.

Rusty continued to squirm. Alan was her cousin, her married cousin. She must be imagining this. It had to be jet lag. She'd never even harbored a long-distance crush on Alan. He'd been her occasional pen pal, her faraway friend, the brother she'd always wanted. She'd been thrilled when he married. Sight unseen she loved Penny, too. What was he doing? And why, in spite of everything, did she like it so much?

Rusty succeeded in pulling away again. She was confused and completely flustered. In her enthusiasm had she sent out signals that she wanted this kind of intimacy? What on earth had she said in all those letters? Had she somehow asked for the kisses that even now filled her body with a sensation as confusing as the kisses had been? "Well," she said, clearing her throat and stepping backward. "Well, uh, we'd better get going. Too bad Penny couldn't come with you. I'm looking forward..."

"Penny?" he asked with a lifted eyebrow and a smile.

"Penny. Your wife." She narrowed her eyes. "The mother of your children."

He dismissed her words with the wave of his hand. "That Penny. What Penny doesn't know won't hurt her, will it?"

Rusty picked up the flight bag that she'd dropped in her burst of enthusiasm. "I'm going to see if I can get a plane back to New York."

Alan began to laugh, and his laughter was loud and musical and distinctly male. Rusty wanted to stuff her flight bag down his throat. When he spoke, the laughter was still in his eyes. "Before you get too charged up, will you let me say something now?"

Rusty nodded warily.

"When you're in the land of Oz, I reckon it's a good idea not to assume anything. Things aren't always what they seem."

"What is this Oz bit?"

"Australia."

"Oh." Rusty listened to him draw out the last word and wondered if her tongue would ever master pronouncing it the same way: Oz-tri-al-yer. "Exactly what do you mean?" she asked, fighting to regain her poise.

"Well, you see, you made a big mistake right off. I'm not your cousin."

"But the T-shirt . . ."

"My name is Daniel Marlin." He grinned engagingly. "I'm a tour guide for Outback Odysseys, too. Alan asked me to meet you. He got stranded up in Alice Springs and Penny is home in bed under doctor's orders." He grinned again with the satisfaction of a man well pleased with himself. "No worries, though. I didn't mind coming to give you a proper hello."

Rusty's amber eyes began to glow—a signal that her friends understood and treated with caution. "'A proper hello'? There was nothing proper about it!"

"No? How about something improper to compare it with?" He stepped toward her, but Rusty's fist placed squarely in the middle of the orange and blue kangaroo stopped him.

"Give me the bad news, Mr. Marlin." Rusty's eyes were flashing fire. "Just how often am I going to have to see you while I'm here?"

His face was only inches from hers. "We ought to make it often enough to improve your disposition."

"Or often enough to improve your manners!"

He laughed and the warmth of his breath brushed her cheek. "Now you're asking for the impossible. I don't spend that kind of time with any woman."

"Oh? Well, I suppose the women in Adelaide are counting their blessings."

"Alan said he thought you'd be a ripsnorter." Daniel casually lifted his hand and brushed a stray curl from her cheek. "It's too bad you're not my type."

She shook his hand away. "Your type would have to have the IQ of a billiard ball and the discretion of a groupie!"

Daniel retreated, examining her as he did. "Not my type, but cute, I'll give you that. Red hair, freckles, button nose, eyes like that jewelry they make out of kauri resin in New Zealand. Old enough to get into my favorite pub, but too young to hold your liquor." He held up his hand to stop her angry interruption. "Quick brain, nasty tongue, and no sense of humor. I'd heard Yanks had no sense of humor, but I didn't believe it till now."

He was despicable. Rusty had heard rumors about Australian men, and in less than five minutes they had all proved true. Daniel Marlin was a typical arrogant male chauvinist, and if she hadn't been so excited about seeing Alan, she'd have spotted him for what he was immediately. She'd seen his kind often enough. New York was full of them, too.

"Our humor would be hard for you to understand," she said as acidly as she could. "You'd have to have a sense of subtlety. Do you understand that word?"

"Right-o. It means the same thing as pompous, doesn't it?"

"Our humor doesn't extend to kissing games!"

"Neither does your talent."

"Mr. Marlin," she said, in tones that matched the fire in her eyes, "if you're any example of the men Australia has to offer, I can see why my mother married an American!"

His blue eyes were just a shade less humorous. "And are you here to carry on the family tradition? Did you think the grass would be greener on the other side of the world?"

"What's that supposed to mean?"

"I suppose you've convinced yourself you came here just to gawk at the scenery."

For a moment Rusty was caught off guard. Just what did he mean? "I came here to see the country," she said carefully.

"How old are you? Twenty, twenty-one?" The smile that accompanied his question was infuriatingly smug.

"Twenty-four."

He nodded as if her answer said it all.

"So?" she challenged.

"Like I said, you're a cute little thing. While you're out there looking at the country, don't you hope you'll run across some rugged, sunburned Aussie man who'll offer you something those city boys in New York couldn't?" He grinned at her sputtering protests. "It's nothing new. We even have American girls advertising in the local rags to meet Australian men. Had one on the telly just the other day. She found her man. Maybe you'll find yours."

There were no words scalding enough to answer him, but Rusty wasn't going to let that stop her. She opened her mouth to tell Daniel exactly what she thought of him when a man's shout behind her destroyed her chance.

"Daniel?" A tall, bearded young man wearing glasses and an Outback Odysseys T-shirt came striding toward them. "And Rusty? Is this Rusty?" Before she could respond the young man picked her up and twirled her around. "Welcome to Australia, Cousin. Welcome home."

* * *

"So anyway, I almost missed her. Would have, in fact, except at the last minute I was able to get an earlier flight from the Alice."

Rusty gazed fondly at Alan, who was explaining their meeting to his wife. Penny was reclining on the living-room couch like a lovely, blond Madonna.

"Lucky for me, she and Daniel were hitting it off so well they were still gabbing when I got there," Alan finished.

"Your cousin was just about to tell me her views on Australian men," Daniel said, his eyes filled with laughter. "Too bad I had to miss them."

"Anytime you want to hear them, Mr. Marlin..."

"Mr. Marlin?" Penny giggled in delight. "Daniel, what did you do to poor Rusty? You're an awful larrikin sometimes."

"My first lesson in Australian vocabulary," Rusty muttered. "Illustrated, yet."

"Cousin Rusty was greeted with all my considerable charm," Daniel reassured Penny. "And I reckon she found me charming. In fact 'gorgeous' was the word you used, wasn't it, Rusty?"

"That was before you opened your mouth."

"You have to understand Daniel," Penny said. "Under all that brass, he's really quite shy."

"A regular shrinking violet," Daniel agreed.

Rusty snorted. "Too bad your ego didn't shrink, too!"

"Phew! I think I'd better open the windows. This place is heating up fast." Alan headed toward ornately carved stairs instead. The Benedicts' home was a bluestone cottage built at the beginning of the twentieth century. The windows were leaded glass, the walls of solid, honey-colored paneling, and the high ceilings were pressed tin. The house was surrounded by carefully tended gardens blooming in spring glory. Rusty had been instantly enchanted. Although they were in the middle of one of Australia's larger cities, it was easy to pretend she was in the English countryside.

Alan stopped at the bottom of the stairs and beckoned to her. "Rusty, come meet your other relative. It's time for him to get up from his nap."

Penny intervened. "Alan, let Daniel get him up and introduce Rusty, would you, darling? I need some help in the kitchen."

"No, that's fine. I'll just wait," Rusty protested as Daniel stood and headed for the stairs.

"Go ahead, Rusty," Penny reassured her, "he's been bonkers about meeting you. There's nothing shy about little Danny."

"Come on, Yank. It's never to soon to tell him your views on Aussie men," Daniel added.

Rusty stopped halfway to the stairs as the significance of her second cousin's name hit her. "Danny... Let me guess."

"My namesake," Daniel said proudly.

She held back all the snide comments that came roaring to mind, directing a question to Alan. "Did you really name your firstborn son after Daniel Marlin?"

"I don't know what he did to you at the airport, honey, but Daniel's really a swell bloke. The best kind of mate."

"A regular saint," Daniel gloated.

Alan smiled at his mate and then turned back to Rusty. "I'm gone so much off on trips, if it weren't for Daniel's help, I don't think I could keep my job. He looks after Penny and little Danny for me, especially now that she's so far along with the next littly."

Although Rusty thought leaving any woman in Daniel's care was the height of naiveté, she didn't voice her thoughts. There was some concept here that she couldn't quite grasp. It had to do with the word *mate*. It wasn't just a substitute for the word *friend*—not the way Alan used it. Obviously, Daniel was more important to him than that. *Mate*—she filed it away on her rapidly expanding vocabulary list to examine later and followed the chuckling Daniel up the stairs.

At Danny's bedroom door she stood and cautiously admired the pink-cheeked toddler clutching a raggedy blanket as he slept soundly, oblivious to everything. Danny had his mother's blond hair, but his face was uniquely his own. Rusty had never spent any time around children; somehow those she'd known in the Big Apple had always seemed to be in the middle of being whisked from one destination to another. Now she wondered what she would say to this tiny relative when he awakened. What did one say to any two-year-old?

Daniel bent over his namesake's bed. "Wake up, sport. Your Dad's home."

Two chubby arms stretched out and two intelligent brown eyes opened to regard the adult looming over him. "Hi, Dan'l," he said seriously, jamming his thumb back in his mouth.

"Cousin Rusty's here," Daniel told him, sitting down on the bed to stroke Danny's hair. "Can you sit up and say hello to her?"

"H'lo," he said with his thumb still firmly in place.

"Hello, Danny." Rusty moved a little closer.

"Her hair's on fire."

Daniel laughed and signaled Rusty to come even closer. "It's just red. Like yours is yellow."

Danny looked as if he wasn't sure Daniel knew what he was talking about.

Rusty cleared her throat. Having Daniel Marlin in the room made this much harder. "Um... Did you have a good nap, Danny?"

"She talks funny."

Rusty smiled. She'd been thinking exactly the same thing about everyone else. "You'll have to teach me to talk like you do."

Danny hid his face in his blanket. "Go 'way."

Whatever Rusty was supposed to say to a two-year-old, she hadn't said it. This obviously was not her day to converse with Australian males.

"I think we'd better let him wake up," Daniel said, standing. "He'll come around when he's ready. And you do take a bit of getting used to."

"I can see where that might be true," she said, following him out of the room. "Especially if you're used to women with brains that fit into teacups."

"I reckon it's not brain size I notice right off." Daniel's eyes dropped just low enough to make his point.

"I reckon you ought to. In any couple, at least one of them should be smart enough to read and write."

Daniel waved off her words. "Some things can be picked up anytime, and some can't be picked up at all." The tone of his voice made it clear what he was referring to and which category he believed Rusty fit into. "I'll take a woman who knows how to treat a man over one with an education any day." Tipping the brim of his hat without removing it, he headed down the stairs. Rusty followed, mentally counting to ten as she descended.

In the living room Penny was straightening cushions and folding newspapers. "I only have to rest for a couple of hours midday," she reassured Rusty who rushed to help. "But I'll bet you're tuckered out—jet lag and all." Penny waved her toward the sofa. "Go ahead and get comfy while I help Alan finish afternoon tea."

Suddenly the sofa looked very inviting. Rusty ignored Daniel's laughter as she slipped off her shoes and did exactly as Penny had suggested. She was a whole day behind. In New York it would be midnight yesterday. That meant she had missed one night's sleep and was about to miss another. At least she thought that's what it meant. Somehow, she was much too tired now to puzzle it out. She leaned her head on the back of the sofa and closed her eyes. It was unbelievably peaceful. It was even possible to imagine that Daniel Marlin was no longer in the room. If she tried really hard she could almost imagine she'd never even met him.

With no intention of doing more than rest for a few moments, she fell asleep.

She was floating somewhere warm and safe. Disembodied voices drifted in and out of her consciousness.

"Poor thing," she heard a woman say, "she was absolutely dead on her feet."

"Well, she sure cracked hardy. I'll give her that," a man's voice answered. "You'd never have known she was so knackered. She's a game little thing."

"Just what did you do to her, Daniel? She was having a real go at you there for a while."

"Just gave her something to think about."

The woman's voice interrupted. "You need something to think about, Daniel me boy. Maybe Rusty's just what you need."

"Don't start that, Penny-Dreadful. I'm not looking for a sheila."

"Who said you were?"

"She's not exactly a no-hoper, but she's not my type."

"She's anybody's type. You know she's a model, don't you?"

There was a pause. Then a snort. "I don't know what she models, but it must sell to kiddies twelve and under."

A man's voice drifted in from far away. "I've got Rusty's room ready. Wake her up and let's get her to bed."

"Rusty..." the woman's voice called.

The first man's voice interrupted. "Don't, Penny. I'll carry her up. Seems a fair cow to wake her. Now, don't look at me like that. I'm just trying to get her out of here."

Rusty felt herself lifted gently through the air. She was too exhausted to fight her way back to consciousness. Instead she snuggled against the warmth that seemed to buoy her. Then she felt the warmth leave her. Someone was covering her with a blanket. She turned to her side and listened to nothing except silence.

In the dream that followed she was upside down in a world where people spoke English she couldn't understand and did everything backward. A man in a felt hat kept laughing at her while a blond-haired cherub tied her feet together with a raggedy blanket. In the midst of an escape attempt in which the car she was driving would only run on the wrong side of the road, she pulled herself awake long enough to give a relieved sigh.

Thank goodness it was nothing more serious than a nightmare.

Chapter Two

Adelaide
October 8th

Dear Sly,

Did you know there are actually cities in this world where the sound of birds is louder than the sound of traffic? There's a magpie warbling outside my bedroom window, and just a few minutes ago a flock of rosellas—parrots to you—settled on a nearby gum tree and chattered raucously enough to wake the dead.

The air is fresh, the sun warm, and no, I'm not sorry I came. (I'm sure you wanted to know, didn't you?)

Cheerfully,
Rusty

Rusty looked up from writing Sly's address on the picture postcard of a sulphur-crested cockatoo to find Danny standing in her doorway trailing the inevitable ragged

blanket. Despite her glowing report to Sly, there had been
some moments in the past week when New York had
seemed entirely too far away. She had the distinct feeling
that this was going to turn into another one.

"Hello, Danny."

The little boy took his thumb out of his mouth long
enough to stick his tongue out at her.

"That's naughty, Danny. How would you like it if I did
that to you?"

"Don't care."

Could this little monster really be the son of Alan and
Penny, two of the nicest, most well-mannered people Rusty
had ever had the pleasure to meet? Had naming the child
after Daniel Marlin put some sort of curse on him? Rusty
shook her head in sad disapproval. "If I stuck my tongue
out at you, you wouldn't like it," she assured Danny. "It
would make you feel bad. It makes me feel bad."

"Don't care." He stuck out his tongue again and wig-
gled it at her.

"I can make worse faces than that."

"Can't."

"Can too. See?" Rusty put her fingers in the corners of
her mouth and pulled it into a distorted grin, sticking her
tongue out and crossing her eyes as she did so. She held the
ghastly pose for a long moment before returning her face
to normal. Danny had been replaced by Daniel Marlin, who
was leaning with one elbow against the doorjamb.

She had the wild impulse to repeat the face and see if
Daniel would turn back into Danny. Instead she sat up a
little straighter. Faced with a decision like that, who could
choose?

In the past week she had learned that all she had to do to
assure Daniel's appearance was lose her self-control. If she
did anything even remotely unladylike or embarrassing,

Daniel was always there to witness it. "Where did you come from? And where did Danny go?"

"I reckon Danny's gone to lag on you."

"Can't be any worse than what he usually does," Rusty said philosophically.

"He's gone to tell his mum what you did," Daniel translated.

"The little angel," she murmured. "And you, Daniel, are you going to lag on me, too?"

"Not me. I'm going to walk you down to the Parade to shop for tonight's tea."

His marked lack of enthusiasm was irritating. Since the kisses in the airport, Daniel had made it clear that although he regarded Rusty as a catalyst for his sense of humor, it was the only way he regarded her. He'd told her right away that she wasn't his type, and as if he'd set out to prove it to her, he'd conscientiously avoided so much as an interested glance in her direction. Rusty, who was used to men's unqualified admiration, found Daniel's lack of interest in her surprising.

Not that she cared. Heavens, no. She had changed her appearance and escaped her career as a model just to get away from being appreciated for what was, after all, only skin-deep. No, she didn't really care that Daniel wasn't attracted to her. She just wondered about it, that was all; just as she wondered why he always showed up at the Benedicts' door with a different admiring woman on his arm. Penny's explanation was that Daniel had always been hopelessly attracted to tall, leggy brunettes with empty heads and vacant eyes. He couldn't resist a one. In Rusty's opinion Daniel was trying to work his way through the world's supply as quickly as possible.

Daniel was alone today, but that in no way seemed to have increased her attraction for him. She wondered why he had offered to shop with her in the first place. She stood and lifted her chin regally. "I can find my own way to the Parade."

"Penny asked me to take you."

And that meant it was settled. Rusty had learned a lot about Daniel Marlin in the week she'd been in Australia. He was everything she'd first thought him to be: chauvinistic, supremely self-confident that he was God's gift to women, and an infuriating tease. He was also completely loyal to Alan, Penny and little Danny. There was no favor too great, no task too difficult, where they were concerned. He popped in and out of their home like a living jack-in-the-box. If Penny wanted him to walk Rusty to the Parade, the main shopping area of the suburb the Benedicts lived in, then Daniel would walk her to the Parade, even if he had to drag her kicking and screaming all the way.

Rusty resigned herself to her fate. "Did Penny give you a list of what she wanted us to buy?"

"Penny seems a bit crook to me. I told her you'd be glad to get the doings and make tea tonight."

"Penny's not a crook. What an awful thing to say!"

"Crook. Sick. Ill." He shook his head as if he were explaining himself to an idiot. "Too ill to cook. I thought you could instead."

"Did you, now?" Rusty began to advance toward him. "And why me? Why not you?"

"My speciality's bush tucker. You and Penny being city girls, I thought you'd want something fancier. Of course, if you can't cook..."

Whatever bush tucker was, Daniel was right. It didn't sound fit to serve to anyone, most especially not to a pregnant woman. Who would want to eat a bush anyway? Rusty drew herself up to her full five-foot-five. "I gather you're staying for dinner." She went on at his nod. "You do eat with a knife and fork, don't you? City food won't seem too strange?"

"I won't even lick my fingers afterward," he said with a grin.

It was really too bad about that grin, Rusty decided. It was very easy to stick Daniel in the category of "hopeless male" and leave him there, but that grin defied all attempts to do so. She'd known men who were better looking, and she'd certainly known men who were considerably less irritating, but in all her days, she'd never known a man with a grin like Daniel's. It seemed to be permanently attached to something inside her. When he grinned, she felt a distinct tug, and her common sense didn't affect her reaction at all.

"I'll make fettuccine Alfredo," she said decisively. "My speciality." The words sounded just right, and there was nothing deceitful about them. It wasn't a lie; she had just chosen not to add the words that should have come next: "It's my only speciality."

She wasn't about to explain to Daniel Marlin that she was completely useless in a kitchen. He didn't have to know that her facility with fettuccine Alfredo had only come after agonizing lessons with an Italian chef who had finally given up on teaching her the basics and instead had taken her step-by-step through one simple dinner menu until she could execute it perfectly. Fettucine Alfredo, green salad, garlic bread and ice cream with crème de menthe poured over it had served her well every time she had entertained. She had even developed an excuse in case she was forced to entertain the same person twice. "I remembered how much you liked this the last time," she'd say as if preparing it again had been a special favor.

"Alan and I are just simple bushies," Daniel said, his eyes laughing at her. "You don't have to get that flash."

"Sure I do," she said airily, meaning every word. "Alan and Penny will appreciate my efforts." Silently she prayed that she could find all the right ingredients. She couldn't trust herself to substitute a thing. "Alan's going to be back from Alice in time to eat, isn't he?"

"Supposed to be."

"Since I've been here, he's hardly been home for more than a night or two."

"Alan's a goer all right."

"Tell me, Daniel," Rusty baited him as they walked down the stairs together. "How come Alan works so hard and you don't seem to work at all?"

"Alan's already finished his last tour for the year. He's a bang-up mechanic, so he's doing season maintenance on some of our vehicles. I'm between tours right now. I head off a week from Monday, if everything goes like it's supposed to."

Rusty caught the frown of concern on Penny's face as she looked up from her resting spot on the sofa. "What do you mean if everything goes like it's supposed to?" Penny asked, with no apologies for entering the conversation.

"No worries, Pretty-Penny."

Rusty still wasn't used to watching the complete change in Daniel when he spoke to Penny. The flip egotist was replaced by the concerned, caring friend. At the bottom of the stairs Daniel swung little Danny off his feet and set him on his shoulders. "What say Rusty and I take the little ankle-biter here with us? Then you can get a sleep while we're gone," he said, obviously changing the subject before Penny could ask any more questions.

"I'm preggie, not sick," Penny chided him.

"Very preggie," he pointed out.

"Not for long."

Rusty was philosophically readying herself for the experience of shopping with both Daniels when she saw the adult Daniel turn a distinctly lighter color. "What do you mean, 'not for long'?" he asked. Rusty noticed the wispiness of his voice. He sounded as if someone had punched him in the stomach, and he was stoically trying to ignore it. This was going to be interesting.

"No worries, Daniel, dear," Penny said serenely.

"What do you mean, 'No worries'? I'm supposed to be taking care of you while Alan's gone."

"There's nothing anybody can do at this point. Nature has the whole thing tidily wrapped up."

"You're going to the hospital. Right now."

Penny looked at her watch. "No, I'd say I'm going to the hospital tonight sometime. At the earliest."

Rusty, whose entire knowledge of pregnancy and childbirth had come from watching old movies on late-night television, didn't think Penny's answer was strange, but Daniel turned another shade lighter. "You can't know that," he said firmly. "I'm going to ring your doctor."

"Already done. He and I are old hands at this, you know." Penny caught Rusty's eye and smiled in conspiracy. "Rusty, will you get him out of here for me?"

Outside on the sidewalk Rusty tried to be magnanimous and pass up the opportunity to goad Daniel, but she found her own maturity sadly lacking. "Ah, Daniel," she said softly. "I thought I'd heard you were a cowboy on a cattle ranch before you became a tour guide. Giving birth shouldn't be any big deal to you."

"Stockman on a cattle station," he corrected her, but Rusty could see his heart wasn't in it. "Cows aren't people."

"Don't wanna baby," Danny said from his perch on Daniel's shoulders, thumping Daniel on the head in emphasis.

Rusty found it heartwarming to see Daniel take some of his namesake's abuse.

"You'll like the baby," Daniel reassured the little boy. "I had seven brothers and sisters. We had jolly times."

"Don't wanna baby."

They had reached the Parade and turned on to the wide sidewalk. Rusty looked at their reflection as they passed by the numerous shop windows. They looked startlingly like a family. Mommy, Daddy and the little darling out for a walk. She grimaced at the picture.

They stopped at the greengrocers, and Rusty bought everything she'd need for a salad. At the bakery next door they bought a loaf of long, thin bread, which Daniel called a husband-beater. At the butcher's shop, Daniel stopped, pulling Rusty to a halt beside him.

"This is a good place to buy meat."

"There's no meat on the menu."

"Don't tell me you're a blasted carrot-eater."

"You won't starve."

"I can see why you're so skinny."

She could have told him that she was skinny because for the past three years her livelihood had depended on it, but she shrugged instead. "At least my arteries aren't clogged."

"No, they're collapsing. No blood flowing to hold them open."

Rusty's eyes flashed, but she pushed past him to continue down the sidewalk. "There's an Italian deli on the next block. I can get what I need there."

"I can get what I need right here." Daniel turned back to the little bakery, made a quick purchase, and came out eating a square pastry. Danny, still on his shoulders, was eating one too, dropping crumbs in Daniel's hair all the while.

"Dessert before dinner?"

"Dinner before dinner. It's a meat pie." Daniel held it out to her. "This is what's made Australia great. Now I won't starve no matter what you serve."

Rusty took a whiff and shook her head.

Daniel continued to hold it out to her. "I thought you were half Australian."

"My view on those things must come from my other half."

The Daniels worked on their pies with obvious enjoyment as they followed Rusty to the deli. She had made her purchases and paid before she realized they were still outside standing on the sidewalk. With them was a lovely girl with hair as black as Rusty's was red and with an expression on her face that could only be called adoration.

"He's beautiful, Daniel," she was crowing softly when Rusty joined them. "Don't you just love children?"

Rusty noticed that the girl, who didn't look as if she were out of her teens yet, had never once taken her eyes off Daniel's face. Rusty wondered how she could tell that little Danny didn't look like Godzilla.

"Rusty, meet Amanda," Daniel said politely.

"Hello, Rusty."

Rusty began to worry that Amanda's vision had locked permanently. She was tempted to growl to see if Amanda was even able to look at her. Instead she murmured something polite and watched Daniel herself.

"Amanda's uncle, Bill MacCready, owns Outback Odysseys," Daniel explained to Rusty.

"Daniel's the best guide in the company," Amanda cooed. "Nobody can beat Daniel."

Rusty rolled her eyes, certain that Amanda wouldn't notice.

"I never see you now that Uncle Bill's not around," the girl went on, addressing herself to Daniel. "If I go down to the depot, Aunt Jane puts me to work."

"Me too," Daniel said with a warm smile.

"Aren't you leading the last tour of the season?"

"Right-o."

"I've been talking to Aunt Jane about letting me go."

"Well, I'll look for you."

Rusty and Daniel moved off to leave Amanda staring at the spot where Daniel had been. Down the sidewalk a block, Rusty found that she couldn't ignore what she'd just seen. It had been unbelievable. "Tell me that's never happened to you before," she challenged Daniel. "Please tell me that doesn't happen all the time. I want to believe in the universal sanity of women."

"What are you talking about?"

"Daniel," she mimicked Amanda's husky tones, "I never see you anymore."

"Females find me fascinating," Daniel said with a grin that was even warmer than his usual.

"Here I thought you were the way you were because of your upbringing."

"What do you mean?"

"I thought you were probably a spoiled child. Instead I bet it's women who have spoiled you. You need a wart on your nose or a chipped tooth or something, Daniel. It would build your character."

Daniel eyed three young women who were walking toward them. At just the right moment, he inclined his head and smiled in greeting. Rusty watched the inevitable happen. One young woman giggled, another pulled herself a little straighter and assumed a walk that Marilyn Monroe would have envied, the third looked quickly at her shoe.

"That was nauseating," Rusty hissed, drawing the last word out as long as she could.

"I like women," Daniel said with no apologies. "And they like me."

"If you really liked women you wouldn't bounce from one to the other like a basketball. You can't like someone you don't even know."

"What makes you think I don't get to know them? How many men have you gotten to *know*?"

Rusty heard the peculiar emphasis on the last word. She should have known better than to try straightening out hopeless Daniel Marlin. "I'm talking about something other than a physical relationship. I'm talking about caring and sharing and sticking with someone through thick and thin."

"You've done that, have you?"

"Well, no...." She grimaced at his laughter. "But you've got years on me, Daniel. When I'm as old as you are, I'll be happily settled with the man I love."

"Tell me about it."

She knew it was hopeless to try and explain her feelings, but she tried anyway. "He'll be someone I can really share my life with, someone who doesn't put me in a role and leave me there, someone who believes my rights, my needs are as important as his own."

"I reckon he'll be easy to find."

Rusty suspected she was walking into a trap, but she couldn't help herself. "Why?"

"A bloke with a halo's not right common."

"I wanna walk." Danny began to thump Daniel on the head now that his meat pie was finished.

"I'm not looking for a perfect man." Rusty stopped and waited as Daniel carefully lifted Danny off his shoulders. "Daniel, you have crumbs in your hair."

He bent his head and shook it in her direction. "How about brushing them out for me?"

Why did the idea sound so tantalizing? Daniel really had beautiful hair, thick and shiny and squeaky clean. Touching it would be a pleasure for anyone. Rusty knew, however, that her own enthusiasm was a little extreme. She disciplined herself to do it as quickly as possible. "Actually, I'm not looking for any man," she continued, running her fingers through the sun-lightened strands. His hair felt even better than she'd imagined—warm and silky. Her fingers kept getting lost in it. "I am not on the prowl. I just believe that sometime I'll want a companion..."

"A dog would be less trouble."

She ignored him, and her fingers headed for the final crumbs. "Someone special in my life. Everyone needs that."

Daniel straightened and shook his hair back into place. "Not everyone."

Rusty shrugged. "I'm not trying to make a convert."

"No problem. You're not the first sheila to try and tell me I ought to tie myself down."

"Ah, but I'm probably the first sheila who couldn't care less if you do or not." Rusty gave a flip wave of her hand, and stepped off the curb to head back to the Benedicts'. Daniel's fingers locked on her shoulder, and she cried out in pain and outrage as he forcibly hauled her back on to the sidewalk beside him.

Her next emotion was sheer terror when a car whizzed by at top speed, and she realized that she had been stepping right into its path. She shut her eyes and felt her knees buckle. It was only Daniel's arm that kept her standing.

"I was looking the wrong way," she said in unnecessary explanation.

"You do that a lot."

"No, that was the first time."

"No. You expect things here to be just like they are at home. You expect people to be the same, too. That can get you into trouble, Yank." Daniel loosened his grip. "Feeling better?"

Rusty nodded. "Thank you."

"No worries. I had to save you for that bloke with the halo."

She tried to smile. When the street was empty, she crossed carefully, leaving Daniel and Danny to follow slowly behind.

At the house Rusty discovered that Penny was asleep on the sofa. She went straight into the kitchen for two aspirins and to see if any of Penny's utensils looked familiar. Nothing was quite the same as home, but by taking a few minor risks, she knew she could put together a decent dinner. She hoped it would be the only time she'd be asked to cook when Daniel was eating with them. She wouldn't mind admitting to Penny that she didn't know what she was doing in a kitchen, but her pride would not let her admit the same to Daniel Marlin—even if he had just saved her life.

Alan arrived home halfway through her preparations. Even though he'd been overworked since her arrival, Rusty had found that her cousin was exactly the man she had hoped he'd be. He was warm, caring, and fiercely proud of his family, of which he considered Rusty a natural part. Both Alan and Penny had not only made her feel welcome, they made her feel she was doing them a favor by visiting. Now Alan gave her a kiss on the top of her head and went to the sink to wash his hands.

"I'll help," he offered.

"Don't worry. I've got it under control. Is Penny awake yet?"

"Yes. She went upstairs for a shower. She seems to think the baby might put in an appearance by tomorrow."

Rusty compared his nonchalance with Daniel's near hysteria. "You make it sound so ordinary."

"We've done this once. We're both excited, but we know what to expect. Poor Daniel, though. He's off his brain."

Rusty thought that was a very good description. "He's so fond of you both," she said, tentatively probing for answers. "I don't know if I've ever seen a man more devoted to his friends."

"We've been mates for a long time."

"Just what does that mean, exactly?"

"Just friends."

"It seems to mean more than that. I've got lots of friends, but I don't think I feel the same way about them that you and Daniel feel about each other. I think he'd lay down his life for you or Penny or little Danny, and I don't think he'd have to think twice about doing it."

"I'd do that for Daniel, too."

Rusty was intrigued. "Why? What happened to make you so close?"

Alan began to wash some of the dishes that had accumulated while he told his story. "Daniel and I were ringers together on a cattle station near Lake Eyre back when we were both still teenagers. It's where we met. Lake Eyre's a big, salt lake north of here a good ways, and there's nothing else there—just the lake and a few stations so big you could set some of your New England states inside them. It's a lonely place, but it suited us both fine."

"It's hard for me to imagine."

"You have to get away from the coasts to know the real Australia. It's nothing like this. It's so big..." He swept his hand through the air to demonstrate what he was saying. "You find out who you are out there. I found out quick, and so did Daniel. I was riding the station boundaries one day, riding on a new filly that had just been broken in. I was supposed to spend the night at one of the boundary huts and then go on to the next one the following day. I made good time, so at late afternoon I decided I'd sidetrack a little, ride over to one of the bores..."

"Bore?"

"Wells. We sink 'em deep in the ground and use windmills to pump up the water. That's the only way this country can run so many cattle. Anyway, this bore had been giving us trouble, and I thought I'd check on it. Halfway there I got down off my horse to look at some tracks, and the horse, being new and scenting water, took off without me."

"What did you do?"

"The horse had my water bag, and it was blazing hot. I knew I was in serious trouble. I could go on to the bore, if I could make it, or I could trace my tracks back to the fence and walk on to the hut where water and food were kept. I started back to the fence, walking slow and following the tracks. After a couple of hours, the wind started to blow. Willy-willies started tearing by—"

Rusty stopped him again. "Willy-willies?"

"Funnels of sand, like your tornadoes, but not as vicious. Sand started blowing so I found some scrub where I could wait it out. It was almost dark before it stopped enough so I could start moving. By then I had a raging thirst, my tongue was swollen, and when I stood, the ground felt like it was moving. I started toward the fence, only it wasn't toward the fence at all. I started wandering, and I guess I wandered for miles, because when Daniel finally found me, I wasn't near anything. And I was almost dead.''

"And Daniel found you?"

"I was expected to ring in that night using the radio in the hut. When I didn't, they thought something was wrong with the radio. No one was too worried—no one but Daniel. He was the only one who knew how green I was, and he'd helped me before when I'd hit a bad patch. So he set out that night to look for me. He followed the fence as far as he dared, then camped for the rest of the night. Started out again as soon as it was light. With some hard riding he found me before the sun had finished what it'd begun.''

"I think I understand the word *mate* a little better," Rusty murmured. She felt a surge of warmth for Daniel.

"After that, we stayed together. Knocked around the backblocks, working on this station and on that one. We stuck by each other. When Bill MacCready of Outback Odysseys met Daniel and asked him to come to work for him, Daniel said not unless I came too. I reckon there's no man better than Daniel Marlin.''

"Well, it's a different view of him, I'll give you that." Rusty added the fettuccine to a pot of boiling water and began to grate Parmesan cheese into a stoneware bowl. "Obviously Daniel has redeeming qualities that aren't necessarily apparent at first sight."

"I don't know why you don't like him. Penny thinks he has his eye on you."

Rusty exploded into laughter. "When Daniel has his eye on a woman, his other eye's off exploring for better possibilities. No, thank you. Besides, he's told me I'm not his type, and he sure isn't mine. Penny's just got to have something to think about while she waits for this baby to appear.''

"What can I do?" Penny waddled into the kitchen, surveying the preparations with her Madonna-like smile. "This is going to be great. And I'm starving!"

"Go sit down, we'll finish up," Rusty assured her.

"I have to stay here. Daniel's killing me with kindness in the living room." Penny's smile broadened. "Daniel really needs his own wife to fuss over, don't you think, Alan?"

"Rusty says she's not his type."

Rusty watched with interest as the conversation about her future sailed back and forth over her head.

"She's definitely his type," Penny said with a nod. "Only, he runs so far and so fast every time anybody gets close, he doesn't know what his type is."

"You really can't push him, you know."

"I'm not going to push him, Alan, I'm not a pushy person."

"May I say something here?" Rusty interrupted.

Penny leaned against the table as Rusty walked by to put the colander in the sink. "Of course."

Rusty faced them both, hands on her hips. "Daniel Marlin may be gorgeous, he may be the best mate in the world, he may be loyal and trustworthy and all the things the boy-scout oath promotes, but he is not for me. Now, I know my accent sounds strange and I know my use of our common language is sometimes incomprehensible, but listen carefully." She spoke her next words very slowly. "I am not interested in Daniel Marlin. I do not even think I like Daniel Marlin."

Penny just beamed. Alan was obviously trying not to laugh. When Daniel finally came into the kitchen to find out when tea would be served, he found three sets of eyes examining him. One set was smug, one set was sympathetic, and one set, the amber one, was flashing fire.

Chapter Three

October 12th

Dear Sly,

There was the funniest ad in the Adelaide *Advertiser* yesterday from someone named Sly pleading with someone named Russet to come home. Imagine anyone desperate enough to go to those lengths!

I've got to go. I'm about to become a second cousin again. More later.

Hurriedly,
Rusty

"Shouldn't you be leaving now?" Daniel's voice rang out from the hallway.

"We've got plenty of time, Daniel, dear."

"I don't want to deliver this baby myself!"

Alan's nonchalant drawl sounded as if it were coming from behind a closed door. "If he had to deliver it, he'd do fine. Delivered more calves in his time than your doctor's delivered babies, Penny.''

"Bullo. Can't you get her out of here, Alan? Blast! She's about to have your baby. Stop laughing at me.''

Rusty stuck her head out her bedroom doorway and watched the three adults moving back and forth at strangely different tempos. ''Penny, are you about to have the baby?'' she asked curiously.

"No, dear, not for hours. Daniel's just off his brain again.''

Rusty exchanged a knowing look with Penny, and the next time Daniel strode by she locked her fingers around his upper arm. It was like grasping solid steel. ''Daniel, come into my room and sit down. Leave Penny and Alan alone to finish getting ready. Otherwise the baby might be born here.''

He didn't move, and Rusty knew enough about immovable objects not to pull. She waited, tightening her grip.

"She's inviting you into her bedroom,'' Penny teased. "You wouldn't refuse an offer like that, would you?''

"I'll respect your obvious innocence,'' Rusty told him in tones sweet enough to serve as dessert. ''We can leave the door open if you want.'' She wasn't sure if his mumble was unintelligible because of his accent or because it was meant to be, but when he was finished, he followed her into her room.

"Sit down and make yourself comfortable,'' Rusty invited. ''They'll be gone in a little while. Penny says you intend to stay the night.''

"Danny might need me.''

"He'd die of shock if he found he was alone with me,'' Rusty agreed. ''It might give him a chance to finish me off, though.''

"Never saw the ankle-biter like that with anyone else. Something about you that sets a man's teeth on edge." The words were accompanied by a smile, as his insults so often were.

"Well, when Penny and Alan are gone, you can keep watch by yourself. I'm beat. I wonder why babies always seem to come in the middle of the night?"

"That's how they get your attention."

"It sure got your attention. What were you doing here anyway?" Even for Daniel a visit at midnight was a little unusual.

"Checking on things."

Rusty nodded. Since the night of the successful fettuccine Alfredo dinner, Penny had been having short bouts of labor that disappeared after an hour or two. She had assured everyone it was completely normal, but Daniel had obviously taken it all to heart. Rusty suspected that he'd been driving by the Benedicts' house each night before going to bed to see if there were lights on. Tonight he had hit the jackpot.

"Why are you so tired?" Daniel asked, standing to move to the window and peer out into the night.

"Besides the fact that it's nearly tomorrow?"

"I thought a New York girl'd be used to late nights."

"Not me. I always had to get my beauty sleep or it would show up on camera."

"You really were a model?"

"Hard to believe, huh?" Rusty sat down to address her postcard to Sly. She was beginning to view them as a sort of journal of her trip. She hoped Sly would save them for her.

"Yes and no." Daniel turned to watch her. "You're a..."

"Cute little thing," she finished before he could. "I know, Daniel."

"You don't do much to make yourself glamorous."

"I always hated being glamorous. I'm afraid this is the real Russet Ames."

"Russet? My word, that's flash, isn't it?"

"Flash but real. My mother said I looked like a little russet apple when I was born. And they suspected my hair would be this color because my father's certainly is." She scrawled U.S.A. on the bottom of the postcard and looked up to see Daniel examining her with an unfamiliar intensity. "Something wrong?"

"You would photograph well."

She was strangely uneasy with the compliment. Daniel was easier to take when he wasn't being this nice. "I do photograph well. I never would have made it as a runway model—too short and too unusual. But for some reason the camera changes all that."

"Going back to modeling when you go home?"

She shook her head, although she hadn't really decided what she was going to do. "I don't even want to think about going home. I haven't seen enough of Australia yet."

"What do you want to see?"

"Alan says the real Australia is out there somewhere." Rusty pointed toward the window behind him. "I want to see it before I go."

"You could take one of those deluxe coach tours. See it all behind air-conditioned windows, stay in flash hotels with swimming pools. You'd miss the flies that way, and the heat."

"And maybe miss Australia."

"Maybe."

"We're going now. Pray it's a girl this time." Penny stood in the doorway, a radiant smile on her face. Alan stood behind her, his arms around what had once been Penny's waistline.

"Good luck," Rusty told them both.

"Daniel, I laid in a supply of grog just for this occasion. I thought you'd need it," Alan told his friend.

"Not me. I've got to stay awake and sober in case the ankle-biter gets up."

Alan and Penny were gone in a flurry of goodbyes. Rusty and Daniel, who had followed them downstairs to see them off, stood in the living room afterward and stared at each other. "I could make coffee," Rusty said finally. "It's going to be a long night for you if you stay awake the whole time."

"No worries." Daniel ran his hand through his hair.

"Suit yourself. I'll say good-night, then."

"Don't."

Rusty was almost at the stairs before Daniel spoke. She turned and cocked her head as if she hadn't heard him correctly. "What?"

"Stay and talk to me."

She was so astounded that Daniel was requesting her presence, her exhaustion disappeared. "Talk? Daniel, we don't talk; we fight, remember?"

He shrugged. "We can fight if you'd rather. But stay a while, would you?"

She surveyed the pleading eyes, the sheepish grin, the casually rumpled hair. There was no question about it. This man knew exactly how to get a woman to do anything he wanted. Daniel was many different people, and each one was uniquely appealing. He was a force to reckon with.

"You big softie," she scolded. "All right, I'll keep you company for a while so you won't worry. Sit down and let me get you that grog Alan mentioned. I won't let you fall asleep."

When she returned Daniel was still standing in the same place. He took the can of beer gratefully, and popped the top, taking a big sip before he spoke. "It would take a swag of these to put me to sleep."

Rusty flopped onto the sofa and propped her feet on a stool. "If we're going to keep each other awake, we'd better try talking or fighting or something."

Daniel looked faintly perplexed.

"What'll we talk about?" she prodded him.

He shook his head. "I don't know."

His answer was so ingenuous that Rusty believed him immediately. She suspected that he rarely talked to women, unless it was as a prelude to something else. Just sharing his thoughts with someone of the female sex would be unique for him and probably very interesting for her. Her curiosity was piqued. "Tell me about your job."

"I take tourists into the outback."

"I know that. Tell me about your trips. How many people go? What kinds of places do you see? Why do you do it?"

He joined her on the sofa, turning his head to look at her. "Hasn't Alan told you anything about Outback Odysseys?"

"Alan hasn't had time to tell me much at all. Penny and I have talked about other things mostly."

"We're a tour company. There's lots of tour companies around, but we sell personality. All the guides are chosen for their..." He stopped as if he couldn't think of a way to explain.

"The guides are a mob of larrikins," Rusty said helpfully. "I've heard. The description suits you, but where does Alan fit in?"

"Alan does our coach tours. They're larger and more superficial. I do the four-wheel-drive trips. There's nothing traditional about them. We have a specially built vehicle that can go over any terrain, and that's just what we do. When I guide, I show my passengers the real Australia.''

"Sounds great. Maybe I ought to go on one."

He laughed. "You'd hate it. We camp in the middle of nowhere, dig our own dunnys..."

"Dunnys?"

"Toilets." He laughed at her grimace. "Swat flies, get sunburned, dodge snakes and crocodiles and red-back spiders."

"And people pay for the privilege?"

"Pay well."

"There's no accounting for taste."

"If the company was run right, we could do twice as many tours. There's that many people who want to go."

"Mummy!"

Daniel was out of his chair like a lightning bolt. Before Rusty could say a word he was up the stairs to comfort his namesake. Minutes later he came back down with Danny in his arms. Apparently the night was going to be longer than either of them had anticipated.

Danny took one look at Rusty and burst into tears.

"Now, now, sport," Daniel crooned. "I won't let mean old Rusty hurt you." He tickled the little boy under his chin.

Rusty was used to Danny's animosity, but at the sight of his tears, she wanted to cry, too. "Bring him over here, Daniel," she asked. "Danny, of course I'm not going to hurt you. I love you. You're my little cousin."

The little boy sobbed as if he'd never stop, and even Daniel's petting seemed to upset him. For the first time in her life Rusty had the desire to pick up a child and cuddle him herself. "Danny, everything's going to be all right," she told him as Daniel settled beside her.

"Don't want new mummy." Fresh tears followed Danny's choked-out words. "Go 'way!"

Daniel and Rusty exchanged a long stare. It was finally clear why the little boy had taken such a strong dislike to Rusty. In his mind, her coming and the baby were inextricably entwined. His mother was getting a new child. He must be getting a new mother. Rusty wanted to laugh or possibly cry with relief. "Sweetheart," she said earnestly, not even aware that she'd used the pet name, "I'm not going to be your new mummy. Your mummy is coming back to take care of you. She'll be your mummy and the baby's mummy."

"Rusty's a friend," Daniel continued the explanation. "Your mummy is only gone for a little while. She asked us to take care of you while she's gone, but as soon as she comes back, she'll take care of you. See?"

Big tears continued down the plump, baby cheeks, but Danny's sniffs began to come further and further apart.

"Do you think he understands?" Rusty asked Daniel anxiously.

He shrugged. "Who can tell?"

"Want Mummy," Danny said softly.

"And she still wants you, sweetheart," Rusty reassured him. "She told me when she comes home, she's going to bring a present. Just for you."

"Want present now."

"Got you there," Daniel said with a laugh.

"Think so?" Rusty stood. "I've got something for you, Danny. It's not a mummy present, it's a cousin present. It'll have to do."

When she returned a few minutes later, she wondered about the impulse that had made her buy the plush kangaroo in a local gift store. Whatever it had been—some latent maternal instinct, or just hope that she could bribe

Danny to like her—she was glad she had given in to it. The kangaroo had one joey in its pouch and another one clinging by Velcro to its tail. It had reminded her a little of Outback Odysseys' logo. Now it seemed like a good lesson for the little boy.

"See this?" she asked softly. "This mummy has two babies. One's little and can't do much, so she keeps it in her pouch. But the other one's bigger, and he can do a lot, so he gets to hop around on his own. And this mummy loves them both."

Danny held out his hands, and Rusty put the kangaroos in them. "You keep them," she told him. "You'll have to take care of them, though. They need someone to love them."

Danny climbed off Daniel's lap to make the kangaroos hop around the room, but Daniel stopped him before he could begin. "Tell Rusty thanks," he reminded the little boy.

Danny looked at her and sniffed.

"It's okay, Daniel," she reassured the elder Daniel. "He doesn't have to. . ."

"T'anks." Danny touched her knee with the kangaroo before he left to hop it around the room.

"Poor little guy. No wonder he hated me," Rusty said softly. "I thought maybe I just didn't appeal to children or something."

"Don't know much about them, do you?"

Rusty shook her head. "I was an only child. And we always lived in New York, mostly in places where I was the only child in the building. I had friends at school, but none of them seemed to have younger brothers and sisters, either. Do you know I've never held a baby? I don't even know if I could."

"It's just like carrying a sack of potatoes. Crying potatoes."

"You must have had lots of practice, being one of seven children. Or was that something boys in your family didn't do?"

"My mother died having my youngest brother. After that, all us kids did anything that needed to be done. If we didn't, we didn't survive."

Rusty thought she understood Daniel's concern for Penny a little better now. It was strange, but before this she'd never thought of Daniel as a real person with feelings, just like everyone else. "That rough, huh?" she said gently.

Daniel finished his beer and set the empty can on an end table. "My dad has a station up in the Gulf country, Queensland way. It's not one of the bigger properties—just big enough to keep him from packing it in. But everyone had to be full of go to make it work."

"I'll bet he was sad to lose you."

"I go back up when it's time for mustering or anytime a trip takes me in that direction. I probably spend six to eight weeks a year up there. I've got two brothers who'll never leave, and that's all the station'll be able to support when my dad dies. Me, I grew up knowing I wanted to spend my life going walkabout. And that's what I've done."

"Going walkabout?"

"Moving around from place to place. Like the aborigines. Are you sure you're half Australian?"

Rusty watched with amazement as Danny hopped back across the room and, without seeming to give it a second thought, settled himself on the sofa between the two adults. He leaned against Daniel and closed his eyes. Without a word, Daniel shifted the little boy so that it was Rusty he was against.

"Look at that," she said softly. She moved her arm to drape it over the little boy's shoulders. His eyelids fluttered open, then drifted shut again.

"Looks like you're a hit," Daniel congratulated her.

They sat quietly for a long time until it was apparent that Danny was sound asleep. Daniel scooped him up, kangaroos and all, and took him back upstairs. Rusty was in the kitchen making coffee when he reappeared minus the little boy.

"So tell me how someone who's half Australian can know so little about this country," he said, as if nothing had happened to interrupt their conversation.

"Thirty years ago my father was here on business. He met my mother, married her and took her back to New York. Her parents didn't want her to go, and there were hard feelings. I guess my mother decided that since she wasn't really welcome here anymore, she ought to forget about everything Australian. No one could be more Americanized than Mom is."

"And she never came back?"

Rusty shook her head. "No, but my grandparents did come to see us once. All was forgiven, and my mother was going to bring me back here to visit, but both my grandparents died before she could. Alan's mother, Mom's sister, was always moving around, and it would have been inconvenient to visit her, I guess. No, I grew up without knowing Australia or my relatives. It's too bad, too, because my father didn't have any relatives, either. I guess that's why meeting Alan was so important to me."

The telephone interrupted, and Rusty laughed as Daniel almost pulled the cord out of the wall. She listened and cataloged the expressions on his face.

"No..." *Disappointment.* "I'm not in a flap..." *Denial.* "Well, lay in there..." *Sympathy.* "Right-o..." *False cheer.* He hung up and turned to give Rusty the news, but she held up her hand.

"Let's see if I can translate. The labor stopped and they're coming home. They just wanted to warn you so you wouldn't have a fit when they walked in the door."

Daniel held out his hand for his cup of coffee in answer.

Back in the living room they sat together on the sofa, staring into space. They were still sitting that way when they heard the Benedicts' car pull into the driveway.

"If this isn't the dizzy limit." Penny came into the living room and giggled at the expressions on Rusty and Daniel's faces. "You two look like you're disappointed about something."

"What did the doctor say?" Rusty asked her.

"She said I ought to go home and get a good night's sleep and that it might be another week or two or even more." She stopped and giggled once more. "Then again, it might be tomorrow."

"It is tomorrow." Rusty stood and waved Penny into a chair. "Want some juice or something? I made coffee for Daniel and me. How about you, Alan?" she asked as he walked into the room.

She returned with juice for them both, but when they had all finished, no one made an attempt to go to bed.

"Well, if you keep this up, Penny-Dreadful, I'll miss the big event altogether," Daniel said, clanking his coffee cup as he set it next to the empty beer can. "I'll be off on tour."

"If you get lucky," Alan said darkly.

"What do you mean, darling?" Penny asked her husband.

Rusty caught the quick exchange of glances between the two men. The signal was clear. Whatever Alan had meant, Penny was not to know about it. But Penny had caught the signal, too. "Look, what's going on?" she asked. "You two have been hiding something for weeks. I don't like being treated like some kind of drongo."

The two men were silent.

"Does this have something to do with Mrs. Mac-Cready?"

There was still no answer.

Penny thumped her glass on the table next to Daniel's growing collection. "Fine. I'll call Mary Wells and ask her what's going on."

"Who's Mrs. MacCready? And who's Mary Wells?" Rusty asked with interest.

"Bill MacCready owns Outback Odysseys, but his wife is sort of managing it while he's on, uh...extended holiday," Penny explained. "Mary Wells's husband is a guide for Odysseys, like Daniel and Alan." Penny lifted her chin. "Mary's always told when something's going on. Mary's husband trusts her. Mary's husband believes she's got a brain."

"All right," Alan said, holding up his hand. "Daniel made me promise not to tell you. Talk to him."

"Daniel?"

Rusty actually felt sorry for Daniel. He looked as if he'd like to be anywhere else. "No worries, Penny."

"Daniel!"

There was no laughter in Daniel's eyes when he finally spoke. "Right-o. Mrs. MacCready's tossing everybody out on their ear. No risk for Alan, but I'm probably going to be the next to go."

For a full minute the only noise in the room was the ticking of the clock on the fireplace mantel.

"Oh, Daniel," Penny said finally, a catch in her voice. "Why?"

Daniel shrugged, and Alan answered for him. "You know what a wowser the old gal is, Penny. Now that she's in charge, nobody's getting a fair crack of the whip. She's already fired two of the cooks because they wouldn't toady up to her."

Rusty was bewildered by the unfamiliar slang, but Daniel helped clear up Alan's explanation.

"Mrs. MacCready doesn't want anyone working for the company who isn't all-up straight. She fired Lyn and Jessie because they laughed at her when she told them they couldn't serve wine with meals anymore. She fired Joe Barnes last week when he refused to follow a boss-eyed schedule she drew up." He paused, obviously trying to decide if he should continue. "And she's going to fire me," he said finally, "because I'm not married, and she's heard the ladies like my tours."

"What about Mr. MacCready?" Rusty asked, although she wasn't sure if she should interrupt. "Will he let her get away with all this?"

Alan answered. "Bill MacCready went on holiday to Norfolk Island six months ago and never came back. His wife had nagged him for years about the way he ran Odysseys, and we all think he just couldn't stand it anymore. Now she's having her chance to do things her way, and she's loving every minute of it." Alan turned to his wife. "Daniel and I didn't want to upset you right now, Penny. My job's safe because she's always liked me, and she knows you're about to have another baby. I fit with her image of what Odysseys guides should be. Daniel doesn't."

Penny was obviously upset. "That's not fair! Daniel never mixes business with pleasure, do you, Daniel?"

He grinned at her, but his blue eyes lacked sparkle. "No, I don't, great trial though it is. But she wants married guides or men with steady girlfriends, men she's sure of. She's not sure of me at all."

"She's lucky to have you," Penny said defiantly. "Any company would be lucky to have you."

"If the job's so bad," Rusty said into the resulting silence, "and you're qualified to guide for someone else, shouldn't you be able to find another job with a company that's not being run by a whomper."

"Wowser," Daniel corrected. "Oh, I can get another job, but not at the pay I get now. And changing jobs will affect my credit rating for a while."

"The big problem is that Alan and Daniel have been saving to start their own company," Penny explained. "They're close to being able to quit Odysseys anyway."

"So close and still a million miles away," Daniel said. "And now Odysseys is going to fire me."

"It's a fair cow," Alan sympathized. "If you could just stay on through the summer, we'd probably be able to borrow the rest of the money we need by March."

"Maybe. But unless I do something to convince Mrs. Mac that I'm all right with the ladies, she's not going to keep me on."

"You need a wife," Penny said heavily. "Haven't I been telling you that for years?"

"For years."

"You don't need a wife, you just need to make Mrs. MacCready think you've got one or almost got one," Rusty pointed out, half in jest.

Three sets of eyes focused on her.

"I was just trying to lighten the mood," Rusty said, defending herself.

"No, it's a good idea," Penny said slowly.

"Nobody's going to believe that Daniel has a wife." Alan yawned. "Everyone knows Daniel."

"Not a wife," Penny said, thinking out loud, "a fiancée. If Daniel was engaged to be married, he'd be safe. Mrs.

Mac wouldn't think twice about trusting him. Under that straitlaced exterior beats the heart of a romantic."

"I'm not going to ask some poor sheila to marry me just so I can report it to Mrs. Mac."

"Of course not. The woman would have to know what was going on," Penny said, obviously warming up to her idea. "She'd have to be willing to play along. Oh!" Penny sat up a little straighter.

"What is it, Penny?" Rusty asked, concerned.

"Nothing. Doesn't anybody see what a beaut plan this is? I know it's not honest—not really—but Mrs. Mac's brought it on herself."

"The woman's got kangaroos in her top paddock."

Rusty wasn't sure if Daniel was referring to Penny or Mrs. Mac, but his meaning was clear. One or both of them were crazy. "Do you know anyone who'd go along with you?" she asked him. The idea of Daniel having to pretend he was about to be married appealed to her. She wondered what effect it would have on his attitude toward women. He'd have to stop flirting, maybe even stop grinning.

"There are sheilas who'd marry me if I asked, but no one stupid enough to tie themselves up that way if I didn't really mean it."

"It would have to be somebody no one knew," Penny said, punctuating her statement with another, "Oh!"

"Why's that, darling?" Alan asked.

"Because no one would believe that Daniel was serious about anyone he's dated around here. They'd know he hadn't been seeing anyone for more than a date or two." Penny lifted her eyes to Rusty's and they were full of affection. "Now, if it was someone from far away, another country even, it would make sense, wouldn't it? Daniel could say he's been saving himself for his one true love, someone he met a long time ago."

"Just a minute," Rusty interrupted.

Penny waved her interruption aside. "Someone he's been mad about ever since. He's just been waiting for her to see the light and come to Australia to marry him. It's a beaut story. And if the girl was his best friend's cousin? Well? What could be more perfect?"

"Just a minute," Daniel interrupted.

"Oh!" Penny bent over for a full minute as all conversation stopped.

"Darling, do you want to go back to the hospital?" Alan asked when she sat up again.

Penny shook her head. "Not yet. Don't you see? Daniel and Rusty can pretend to be engaged. Rusty's going back to the States sometime, but probably not until Daniel doesn't need the job anymore anyway. It won't hurt anybody. It will just ease Mrs. Mac's mind."

"What about my mind?" Rusty stood up and pointed her finger at Daniel. "What about his mind? We can't even stand to be in the same room together! No, this won't work. Absolutely not!"

"She's right." Daniel stood, too. "No one would believe I wanted to marry Rusty anyway."

Rusty turned to him, her eyes shooting fire. "What do you mean no one would believe you wanted to marry me? They'd all say you were lucky to get me! The problem is that no one would believe I'd settle for someone like you, Daniel Marlin!"

"But nobody knows you, Rusty," Penny pointed out.

"Do I look sane? That's all they'd need to know. No sane woman would want this man!"

"There are women all over Australia who want him." Alan stood and crossed the room to kneel at Penny's feet.

"Then Australian womanhood needs its consciousness raised!"

"If he were engaged, he'd be out of the picture. Think what that would do for women." Penny gasped and bent over again.

"I ought to say I'll do it just to make you tow the line," Rusty said, turning back to Daniel. "Somebody needs to whip you into shape."

"Not much chance you'd manage it."

They glared at each other until Alan stood and broke the tension. "I'd say you two will have to finish this alone. Penny and I have another date with the doctor."

"You two stop all the argy-bargy," Penny said, standing to hang on to Alan's arm. "Rusty, I know Daniel's a bit of a pain in the neck sometimes, but he's really not a bad lot. It's not like you're interested in anyone else, is it?"

Rusty shook her head reluctantly.

"If you did this, it would be helping Alan, too. He and Daniel have worked so hard to get their own company going."

Rusty groaned. She could hold out against almost anything except guilt.

"And Daniel, how can this hurt you? Maybe it would slow you down a little, but that's all. And you'd have your own company. Think of that!" Before anyone could say anything, Penny added the clincher. "Think of this baby, Daniel. Think of little Danny." She smiled serenely. "Think of their futures."

This time Daniel and Rusty groaned in unison.

"Take your time," Penny said, bending over again. "I'll wait until you decide."

"Is she always like this?" Rusty asked no one in particular. "Does anybody ever have a chance against her? And I thought she was so sweet."

Alan straightened and held his hands out helplessly. "Would someone please start boiling water?"

"All right! We'll pretend we're engaged," Rusty and Daniel shouted together.

"But it's just an act," Rusty warned Daniel, facing him with her hands on her hips. "Don't you get any ideas!"

"No worries, Yankee girl. The kinds of ideas I'd get about you wouldn't threaten a ruddy hair on your head."

"I'll call you as soon as there's news," Alan said from the doorway. But by then Daniel and Rusty were so involved in another argument they didn't even hear him.

Chapter Four

October 18th

Dear Sly,
And to think that according to the newspapers you're shivering in the middle of the coldest fall on record! Yesterday I sunned myself on a rocky beach and later I picked wildflowers while I watched baby lambs romp in a bright green meadow. Ah, spring!

I've got to go now. The reflected light from the diamond on the fourth finger of my left hand makes it hard to see this card. Catch you later.

Sentimentally,
Rusty

A loud banging on the door of her bedroom made Rusty look up from the desk. "Come in."

"Are you ready yet?" Daniel threw her door open with a bang and stood in the doorway with his arms crossed over his chest and his foot tapping.

"Why Daniel, darling. How nice you look," Rusty purred. "Any girl would be thrilled to be seen with you today."

"You're trying to make me sick, aren't you?"

"Why Daniel, darling, what a way to talk to the little woman who's going to share your life." Rusty stood and twirled slowly around the floor so that he could admire her. "Won't Mrs. MacCready love me? Aren't I just what she ordered for you?"

The rainbow-hued gathered skirt billowed around Rusty's calves as she twirled, and one strap of her lace-trimmed yellow camisole slipped down over her shoulder provocatively. She was the picture of sweet femininity. She had even tied a wide yellow ribbon around her unruly cluster of red curls to complete the picture. The look wouldn't do for the pages of *Vogue* magazine, but it was perfect for the Outback Odysseys' annual spring picnic.

"You're a real beaut. Now come on."

"In such a hurry to be with me," she trilled sweetly.

"Doesn't she look lovely." Penny came through the hallway to stand next to Daniel. "You've made such a wise choice, Daniel dear."

"Are you sure you won't come, Penny?" Rusty smiled at her cousin-in-law fondly. "Your mother said she'd babysit. It might do you some good to get out for an hour or two."

"You'll understand someday. I just can't leave the baby yet. She's so new."

"Almost a week." Julia Rose Benedict, six pounds, ten ounces, had been born the morning of Rusty's ersatz betrothal to Daniel. Daniel said that Julia was the only good thing that had happened on that day. Rusty agreed. It was the only thing she and Daniel had agreed on since.

"Well, at least Alan and Danny will be at the picnic," Daniel said heavily. "There'll be someone to talk to."

"Why Daniel, darling, you know you can always talk to me." Rusty slipped her hand through his arm and gazed adoringly up at him. "I worship at your feet."

Penny's giggles filled the hallway with music. "Good on ya, Rusty. He merits some ragging."

"Pack it in, Penny-Dreadful." Daniel pulled his arm from Rusty's grip. "Let's go and get this over with."

Rusty winked at Penny and followed Daniel outside to his car.

"You get in on the other side, remember?" Daniel stood by the passenger door ready to help her in. "Or did you want to drive the car as well as drive me crazy?"

"Sorry, I keep forgetting you Aussies do everything backward." Rusty joined him and let him help her into her seat. She could fault Daniel for almost everything else, but his manners were excellent. There were women who would find his deference to the fair sex discriminatory, but Rusty found it pleasant. And she had to admit that Daniel's touch on her arm as he helped her in was pleasant, too.

The four-wheel-drive wagon hummed a lazy song of leashed power as they drove toward the park where the picnic was to be held. Rusty stole an occasional glance at Daniel. He really did look nice today. He was wearing white moleskin trousers, like those that she'd been told stockmen often wore, and a subtle plaid shirt with the same brown as the felt of his hat. His elastic-sided boots matched his braided kangaroo-hide belt, and the effect was altogether pleasing and masculine. Sly would be able to find him a job in a heartbeat. Men's cologne, or cigarettes, or maybe...

"Now, don't lay it on thick when we get there."

The hostility in Daniel's tone destroyed Rusty's growing sense of well-being. She sniffed. "Don't tell me what to do. I'm the one who makes her living pretending she's something she's not. I'll do fine."

"Just don't go waving that ring in Mrs. Mac's face right off. She'll get suspicious."

"Too bad this picnic finally got scheduled, isn't it? You thought you'd leave on your trip and get away with not even having to be seen with me."

Daniel shrugged. His eyes never left the road. "This'll put an end to it. One appearance together is all it will take."

"I know what's bothering you, Daniel, darling," Rusty chided him. "This is going to cramp your style. Now everyone will know that you've got a sweet young thing waiting to marry you. All those poor, poor, heartbroken Australian sheilas will see this ring and fall despondently by the wayside."

"Let's just hope that none of those heartbroken Australian sheilas notice that the ring belongs to Penny."

Rusty examined the small opal surrounded by tiny diamond chips. "We can just tell them we liked hers so much we wanted one exactly like it."

The park that Mrs. MacCready had chosen for the picnic was just one of many such parks ringing the city of Adelaide. Green space had been a priority when the city had been designed, and even the nearby hills had huge sections set aside as conservation areas. Daniel parked his car and came around to open Rusty's door.

The Outback Odysseys spring picnic was a tradition that had begun five years before. Since the staff was small—and quickly growing smaller—there was little reason for such a celebration just for themselves. But Bill MacCready had gotten the idea of inviting all his former guests to come and have a yearly reunion with friends and staff they had met on their trips. The idea had been an instant success, in both the goodwill it generated and the number of former passengers who signed up for more trips for the following season. An afternoon of barbecuing sausages and drinking beer out in the sunshine stimulated glorious memories.

This year's picnic, without Bill at the helm, was doomed to be a disaster. Mrs. MacCready had organized it, cancelled it and reorganized it enough times to take all the spirit out of it. When it had finally been set for this Saturday, Alan and Daniel had spent days trying to come up with reasons not to attend, but both had finally given into the inevitable. And now, as a way of announcing Daniel's engagement and presenting Rusty to Mrs. MacCready, it was much too good an opportunity to pass up.

"Looks like there are quite a few people here." Rusty slid off the high seat and stood in front of Daniel.

Daniel shut the door, then pinned her against it by putting an arm on either side of her head. "Now look, Rusty, are you going to play this straight?"

His face was only inches from hers, and at that proximity, she found it strangely difficult to be flippant. "I know this is important."

"Too right it is. Alan's future depends on it as well as mine."

"Why do you think I'm doing this? Besides the sheer joy of making you squirm."

He threaded the fingers of one hand through her curls. Anyone watching would have believed it had been done in affection. Only Rusty felt the menacing tug. "Two can squirm."

"Aren't you being a bit heavy-handed?"

Daniel bent toward her, and before she could decide just what he was trying to do, his lips met hers. The kiss was over almost as soon as it had begun. "Maybe a bit," he said as though nothing had happened. "I just don't want you to queer this for Alan or for me."

"Why did you do that?" she asked, trying to breathe normally.

"Because Mrs. MacCready is on her way over here. Ready?"

She tried to find a smile somewhere inside her for the occasion. "Are you going to tell her we're engaged?" she asked softly.

"Just as soon as the time is right." Daniel slipped his arm around Rusty's shoulders and pulled her along the sidewalk. "Hello, Mrs. Mac," he said politely. "I'd like you to meet a friend of mine, Rusty Ames. Rusty, this is Jane MacCready."

"How do you do," Rusty murmured. She understood immediately why Alan and Daniel called this woman the Iron Maiden. There was nothing important about her that wasn't gray. Gray hair, gray eyes, grayish complexion. Her dress was gray, her shoes were gray. Even the silver bracelet she wore was tarnished to a pewter hue.

"How do you do." Mrs. MacCready examined Daniel through narrowed eyes. "Did you meet Miss Ames on one of your trips?"

"No, Rusty and I have known each other a long time. She's Alan's cousin."

"You're the one from America?" she asked, turning back to Rusty.

"That's right. New York."

"A big, ugly city."

Rusty swallowed twice before answering. "Very different from Adelaide."

The corners of Mrs. MacCready's mouth turned up. The movement surprised Rusty so much she forgot her animosity. "I like New York," the older woman confessed, "even if it is a big, ugly city. I had my honeymoon there."

Rusty smiled too. "A very wise choice."

Mrs. MacCready nodded and continued on her way.

"She's not so bad. Why didn't you tell her?" Rusty asked Daniel, tugging on his arm to keep him beside her a moment.

"What do I say? Hello, Mrs. Mac. Here's my new fiancée. Can I keep my job now?"

Rusty had to admit it did sound suspicious. "I just want to get this over with so we can go home."

"Right-o. Well, we'll do it as soon as we can. We'd better party on now." Daniel took Rusty's hand and linked his fingers through hers.

Walking side by side with their hands clasped, Rusty had the oddest illusion that neither she nor Daniel was living a lie. It was a day made for lovers. The sun shone brightly overhead in a sky as blue as Daniel's eyes. The park, too, was ablaze with spring color. Red bottlebrush trees swarmed with chattering lorikeets whose green and red bodies were nearly camouflaged by the foliage. Gray and rose galahs sailed overhead, landing in the high tops of white-barked gum trees to call to each other over the noise of the shouting humans. The air smelled fresh with the faint scent of eucalyptus and the last remnants of golden wattle. For a moment, Rusty could almost imagine that she was in love with the man next to her and that the beautiful spring day had been made for them.

The moment didn't last long.

"Daniel. I wondered when you were going to get here." Raven-haired Amanda, wearing shorts so tight they appeared to be painted on her soft white skin, took Daniel's free arm and linked her hand through it. "Now the fun can begin."

"Amanda, do you remember Rusty?" Daniel asked.

"G'day, Rusty."

Rusty had been practicing her Australian for just such a moment. "G'day," she answered.

"Hey, that was right well-done," Daniel complimented her.

"Ta," Rusty said modestly.

"That, too. We're going to make an Aussie of you yet."

Amanda appeared not to have noticed the exchange. "Daniel, do you remember last year's party?"

"Not clearly."

"You and I won the three-legged race."

"So we did."

"Will you be my partner again?"

"Rusty..."

"Rusty is wearing a skirt. She won't want to be in it."

Rusty thought the truly amazing thing about Amanda's statement was that the girl knew what she was wearing. As on their last meeting, Amanda hadn't looked at her even once. "Go ahead, Daniel," Rusty said lovingly, "have your fun while you can. When you're an old married man, no one's going to want to be your partner anymore."

Amanda laughed uncertainly. "Daniel?"

"Right-o."

"I'll catch you later, then." Amanda trotted off toward the barbecue area.

"How many Amandas are going to have their hearts broken today?" Rusty squeezed Daniel's hand. "Ten? A Hundred?"

"I don't ask the female sex to throw themselves at me."

"That grin asks them to. Those eyes ask them to."

Daniel dropped her hand and pulled her up against his side, resting his hand on her hip. "And you're immune?"

"Thank heavens."

His thumb slipped between the camisole and skirt to caress her waist. "I wonder."

"Wonder all you want."

"Models lead a right fast life, don't they?"

"Only in sleazy novels."

"I reckon there's some basis for those stories."

"I reckon there's some basis for the slap you're going to get if you don't move that thumb."

"Too clever by half, aren't you?" Daniel's thumb resumed a more normal position.

"You've already proved I've got nothing to worry about from your kisses. But keep your hands to yourself if you want me to continue this charade." Rusty smiled brightly as she muttered her threats. They were nearing the group. On the edge she saw Alan with Danny on his shoulders, talking to several other men.

"You've got no idea what a kiss really is, Yank. If I'm ever stuck for something to do, I might show you."

"Catch me sometime before I'm going to bed. It might help put me to sleep." Rusty covered Daniel's hand and pulled it away from her side. She suspected she would have a bruise in that spot tomorrow. "Alan, Danny, hello. Isn't this a gorgeous day? I'm sorry we couldn't get Penny to come."

Rusty smiled warmly as Alan and Daniel introduced her to the other guides. They were, she decided, the mob of larrikins she'd been warned about. No group of men she'd ever encountered was more overflowing with individuality. She was passed from one to the other and examined carefully. Alan and Daniel had decided not to let anyone know that Daniel's engagement was a sham, and judging by the alert eyes that flicked to her left hand, Alan had already announced Daniel's new status to his cohorts. Obviously, they now were deciding whether Daniel had made a good choice or not.

Daniel stood off to one side and watched.

"Daniel, you know what they say about redheads," one older man who'd been introduced as Noel Wells, said finally.

"Every bit of it's true," Daniel drawled.

"If you can't handle her, send her my way."

"If I can't handle Daniel, where do I send him?" Rusty asked politely.

"To the devil," Noel answered, and all the men laughed.

Rusty laughed, too. "I thought he'd already been there and back."

"She'll do," Noel affirmed. "She'll make you a good missus." He clapped Rusty on the shoulder. "He gives you any trouble, give it right back."

"She does." Daniel came up and lay his arm over Rusty's shoulders. For a moment he almost seemed proud of her.

More introductions followed. Rusty was surprised to see how many former guests Daniel knew by name. It was apparent that he had excellent people skills. He was friendly, but he never crossed the line into false intimacy. He was polite, interested in what was said to him, and unfailingly good-humored. His attitude toward the women who had been on his trips was especially interesting. His smile and his eyes were always warm, but he kept a part of himself back, too. For the first time, Rusty was certain that when Daniel said he never mixed business with pleasure, he was telling the truth.

They ate sausages, which Rusty found delicious, and a variety of salads. The soft drinks Mrs. MacCready had substituted for beer were cold, the sun warm, and the company a mixture of both. Rusty could almost see the rumor about her engagement to Daniel spreading through the crowd. The guides and their wives were openly friendly to her, some of the former female passengers were not.

Inevitably, it was Amanda who first asked if the rumor was true. Rusty, with Danny in her arms, was watching Daniel and another guide move more tables to the area when Amanda approached her.

"So Daniel's going to marry you."

Rusty looked up to see that Amanda still wasn't looking at her. Her eyes were trained on Daniel's movements. With difficulty, Rusty stifled a laugh. "That's right."

"That's lucky for you."

"You could say it's lucky for him," Rusty said, trying to raise Amanda's consciousness a little. It was never too early to start. "Why is it always the woman who's supposed to be lucky?"

Amanda smiled and looked Rusty straight in the eye. "Because the man is Daniel Marlin, and anyone would be lucky to have him," she said. Her words were said in the worshipful tone that Rusty had playfully used with Daniel earlier. The difference was that sweet young Amanda wasn't kidding. "Daniel's one of a kind," the girl continued. "But then you must know that."

Rusty thought Amanda's last statement was one she could wholeheartedly agree with. "He is that."

Amanda sighed. "Do you mind if I borrow him just this once for the three-legged race? It's as close to him as I'm ever going to get."

"Be my guest."

"I wouldn't be so generous if he were mine."

"I know I've got absolutely nothing to worry about." Which was true, of course, but Rusty knew Amanda wouldn't understand why.

She continued to stand on the sidelines after Amanda wandered off. Danny got down to play with some other children. Those adults and older children who wanted to were participating in relay races and contests of skill, all proceeding with much hilarity and enthusiasm. Daniel was helping with the organization of different events, but in between he came to her side to play the role of adoring fiancé. They stood with their arms around each other's waists, like lovers who are so content in their intimacy they have no need to prove anything. Rusty decided that the day hadn't been too bad, after all. If the worst thing she ever had to suffer for Penny and Alan was an afternoon of Daniel's arm around her, then she could manage it stoically.

Her stoicism ended abruptly at the start of the three-legged race.

"I'm ready, Daniel," Amanda said, coming up to drag Daniel away from Rusty.

"Good luck, darling," Rusty said, standing on tiptoe to peck his cheek. "I hope you win this year, too."

She watched Daniel begin to tie his leg and Amanda's together with two soft cords. It was obviously not a job he disliked. Was she imagining it or did his hands linger just seconds too long each time he touched his pretty young partner?

"Daniel always seems to enjoy this event." Mrs. Mac-Cready, who had spent most of the afternoon running back and forth taking care of details, came up to stand beside Rusty. "Usually he enjoys it in the company of his date," she said disapprovingly. "Not my niece."

"Oh, I wasn't dressed for it," Rusty explained. "Amanda was. Besides, I understand they won together last year."

"Humph."

Rusty could think of no reply.

"I don't like my guides paying special attention to any of the guests. Especially my unmarried guides. And especially not Amanda."

"I'm sure Daniel pays just enough attention to be sure everyone is having a good time," Rusty said uneasily.

"He's too available." Mrs. MacCready humphed again.

Rusty knew her chance had come. She tried to sound nonchalant. "Oh, Daniel's not really available at all."

Mrs. MacCready refused to take the bait. "That's what he always tells me, but look at him now."

The race had begun. With their arms around each other's waists, Daniel and Amanda were sprinting toward the turnaround.

"They do look like they're having fun."

"Humph."

Amanda and Daniel rounded the turn and started back. They were in second place when the accident occurred. Amanda, whose grace and coordination had been remarkable, suddenly seemed to stumble. She fell, and Daniel, despite his best efforts, fell with her. Rusty watched in astonishment as Amanda twisted so that Daniel landed on top of her. They lay together like a sandwich with no filling while the onlookers roared with laughter.

This time Mrs. MacCready's "Humph" was like the trumpeting of an elephant. "He did that on purpose."

Rusty might have her own dark suspicions about Daniel Marlin, but she could not believe that the woman beside her would interpret what had just happened as having been Daniel's fault. The pretty teenager had orchestrated the whole thing. "Of course he didn't," she said indignantly, forgetting that Mrs. MacCready held Daniel's and Alan's futures in her hands. "Amanda did it. And I know why!"

"It's obvious Daniel did it."

"That's ridiculous. Daniel's practically a married man. Amanda's just testing her powers, like any girl that age would do. Too bad it's not going to work!" Rusty marched across the field in front of her and to the applause of the crowd, pulled Daniel from Amanda's clutches. She yanked the cords binding their legs free and helped him stand. Then, in full view of everybody, she stood on tiptoe, wrapped her arms around his neck, and said in a voice loud enough to carry a mile, "Tough luck, darling." Then she kissed him.

It wasn't a kiss like any of the others they'd shared. She wasn't startled this time, or embarrassed. She was simply determined to prove to everyone there, including Daniel, that no one could possibly be competition for her. She kissed him, and when his arms tightened around her waist and he pulled her against him, she continued kissing him until her head felt a pound lighter and her feet were inches off the ground.

When she finally pulled away, she tried to smile. "That should compensate you for not winning."

For once, Daniel seemed to have nothing to say.

"May I see you two over here, please?" The icy tones of the Iron Maiden brought them both out of their paralysis.

With a quick glance Rusty saw one of the guests helping Amanda to her feet. The dark-haired girl was giggling. With Daniel's hand firmly in hers, Rusty pulled him to stand in front of Mrs. MacCready.

"Have I missed something?" the older woman asked them.

Rusty ran through her repertoire of facial expressions and decided that "confused" would be in order. Daniel seemed to be thinking along the same lines. "Pardon me?" he said politely.

"Are you two getting married?" Mrs. MacCready came directly to the point.

Rusty tried to blush, but it was beyond her talents. She settled for a tremulous smile instead. "Yes, we are."

"When?" The question was asked without so much as a twinkle in the Iron Maiden's eye.

"We haven't set a date," Rusty said, sticking to the line she and Daniel had agreed on.

"Soon." Mrs. MacCready was obviously sizing them both up. "Better be right away."

This time Rusty's widening eyes had nothing to do with her training as a model. "Why?"

"You're obviously in love. Why wait?"

"Well, Daniel's got his job to think about...."

"Yeah, my job," Daniel agreed.

Mrs. MacCready waved aside their words. "Nonsense. You get married, Daniel, and it will help your job. Big weddings are a waste of time and money. There's no need to wait. No reason at all. How long have you known each other?"

Daniel and Rusty stared. "Um...four years," Rusty said finally.

"That's too long. If you wait much longer, you won't want to bother." She glared at them. "I can't have my guides engaging in any hanky-panky, you know. We have a reputation to keep up here."

"Hanky-panky?" Rusty straightened her spine.

"I run a tight ship. I want good, solid, married men working for me. Now I'm going to feel a lot better about you, Daniel, if you tie the knot, especially with Amanda going on your next trip."

"Amanda's going?"

"It's going to be a gift from me. She wants to get away from her mother for a while, decide what she's going to do with her life."

"I'm not going to get married to suit you, Mrs. Mac-Cready," Daniel said. His voice was soft, but Rusty felt it penetrate to the center of her. Without a doubt Daniel was about to tell Mrs. MacCready what he thought of her—and lose his job.

"What Daniel means," Rusty said hastily, "is that our getting married is a personal thing. We're getting married because we love each other, and we want to spend our lives together. We'll get married as soon as we can be together for a nice long honeymoon. I don't want to marry Daniel and have him go off and leave me right away. That would be no way to start a marriage."

"Go with him, then."

Rusty couldn't think of a thing to say.

"Take it from me, girl, go with your man. Do what he loves best. I wish I'd done more of that when I had the chance." The Iron Maiden seemed to melt a little. "Is there any reason you can't marry him this weekend?" When neither Daniel nor Rusty answered right away, she went on, and her voice got more and more sentimental as she continued. "Life's too short to spend any of it waiting. Daniel, take Rusty with you, show her your world. What better way to bind you together?"

Daniel's answer was a cross between a choke and a wheeze.

"We can't," Rusty protested. Her thoughts were whirling and she grabbed the only one that seemed logical. "Daniel's got a job to do. I'd only be in the way."

"Well, dear, that's easily solved." Mrs. MacCready turned a little so that she was facing Daniel head-on. "Do you remember I told you I was going to hire a new cook for your tour? Well, I think I just found you one: Mrs. Daniel Marlin.''

Chapter Five

October 26th

Dear Sly,

If you were going on a camping trip, would you mind eating fettuccine Alfredo for fourteen nights straight?

My new husband and I are "going bush" tomorrow, along with a dozen other crazies. And you thought Central Park was dangerous! If my ashes make it back to New York, would you please have them sprinkled over Times Square?

Resignedly,
Rusty

"Who do you send all those postcards to?" Penny watched Rusty drop Sly's latest card in the mail slot at the post office. "You're a married woman now. Is this someone Daniel should be jealous of?"

Rusty looked both ways and pulled the hood of her raincoat tighter around her red curls. "The cards are to my agent. I'm not a married woman. And if Daniel saw me standing on that corner in a passionate clinch with Robert Redford, he wouldn't bat an eye." She surveyed the scenery once more before stepping from beneath the shelter of the post-office overhang. "Wouldn't it be terrific if Mrs. MacCready drove by right now? I'm supposed to be home in bed with Daniel this weekend."

"You'd be up a gum tree, all right."

"What a strange place for a honeymoon."

"Up a gum tree. In trouble," Penny translated. "Don't worry though, it's a rainy Sunday. Mrs. MacCready's probably home plotting how next to strengthen the moral fiber of Outback Odysseys now that she thinks she's got Daniel married off." Penny joined Rusty in the light drizzle. She was pushing Julia Rose, who was sound asleep in a pram with a transparent plastic rain shield. Danny, dressed in a bright yellow rain slicker, was walking by her side.

"If she only knew the truth. Where do you suppose my dear husband is at this moment?"

"Keeping a stool at the pub warm."

"I wonder if that's where he spent his wedding night, too."

Penny leaned over to adjust the rain shield. "Actually, Daniel's probably at home right now getting ready to leave tomorrow. He makes it look like he's a larrikin, but nobody works harder than Daniel."

Rusty had spent enough time at the Outback Odysseys depot during the past week to know that Penny wasn't exaggerating. When it had become apparent that she and Daniel would either have to go on the tour together or tell Mrs. MacCready the truth, neither Rusty nor Daniel had chosen to opt for honesty. They had spent hours trying to think of a way to get out of the trap they had set for themselves, but nothing had materialized. The specter of Daniel's dismissal had haunted them both, and in the end, Rusty had agreed to go on the tour as Daniel's pretend wife. Supposedly they had been married yesterday in a quiet, romantic ceremony with only Alan and Penny as witnesses.

The decision hadn't been entirely unselfish. Rusty had wanted to see Australia. If she hadn't wanted to do it this austerely, neither had she wanted a deluxe tour. She had wanted adventure—that had been her primary reason for the trip to Australia in the first place. Going to the Outback as Daniel's pseudo wife was certainly going to be an adventure. For that matter, cooking breakfast, lunch and dinner for fourteen people was going to be an adventure, too. She only hoped they all survived.

"You're very quiet." Penny turned to Rusty as they waited for the light to change to cross the street. "Are you sorry you got yourself into this?"

"Got myself into it? It seems to me you had something to do with this. Tell me, Penny-Dreadful," she saw Penny wince at Daniel's favorite nickname for her, "did you set this up as a matchmaking attempt? I'm not blind to all the times you've tried to throw me together with Daniel."

"If I'd plotted for weeks, I couldn't have come up with such a grand scheme."

The light changed and they crossed the street. Rusty helped Penny lift the pram over the curb, then took Danny's hand. In the few weeks she'd been in Australia she'd become amazingly domesticated. The children no longer seemed strange to her. Now Danny routinely crawled up in her lap to hear stories, and she'd even walked the floor with Julia Rose to give Penny some free time.

Rusty continued the conversation once they were moving again. "Aside from the fact that I now have to spend two weeks in Daniel's company, I do feel bad that we're lying this way."

Penny giggled. "You could have gotten married. I did suggest it. Then none of this would have been a lie."

"No, then it would have been a disaster. A bigger disaster than it already is," Rusty amended.

"Who knows what will come of two weeks in Daniel's presence?"

"Nausea, heartburn, terminal boredom."

"I don't know how you can say that, but think of it this way: if you don't want to be a model anymore, after this trip is over you'll have experience as a camp cook and hostess."

Rusty wanted badly to confess her lack of cooking skills. She had hinted all week that she didn't feel qualified to cook for a crowd, but Penny, who had served as Alan's cook once or twice before Danny was born, had only laughed. "Anyone who cooks as well as you do, Rusty, will do just fine," she'd said.

Rusty hadn't had the heart to admit that except for the fettuccine Alfredo, which she'd served the Benedicts twice, every other meal that she had taken responsibility for had been prepared by a local catering company and transferred to Penny's pots and pans for reheating. Even at that, she'd burned an entire casserole of sweet-and-sour chicken, which she'd had to bribe the caterers to replace. Now, a combination of pride and shame made it impossible for her to admit what she'd been doing. One thing was for certain: when this trip to Australia was over, she would be so scrupulously honest for the rest of her life that her nickname would be Trusty Rusty.

"Well, maybe I'll be an experienced camp cook by the time I get back," she told Penny as they neared the Benedicts' house, "but while I'm getting that experience, I hope the passengers don't starve. I can't imagine cooking over a fire or filling up all those huge pots and pans with food." She thought of the kitchen equipment that Daniel had shown her on one of the trips into the depot. And she'd been confused using Penny's pots and pans! What was she going to do with pots large enough to make soup for everyone in Manhattan?

"I've told you. Just take your usual recipes and multiply them by four. After all, this is a comparatively small tour. Subtract a little liquid, add fewer herbs and spices until you've tasted everything. You'll do fine. You know you have to use a lot of tinned food, I heard Daniel telling you that. You can shop in some of the towns you'll go through, but mostly you'll have to rely on what you bring with you. Just keep it simple."

Rusty had haunted butchers' and greengrocers' and supermarkets for the past week with a cookbook in one hand and a calculator in the other. Every waking hour had been spent trying to figure out how to feed an army of fourteen. Some of the preparations were simple enough, even for her, but when it came to figuring how much meat she'd need to serve, or how many potatoes she'd need for mashing, she was operating on faith alone.

"Well, it will be simple enough," Rusty said heavily. "*Primitive* might be a better word."

"Good plain bush tucker. Just be sure to give them billy tea and damper every night before going to bed, and you'll keep everyone happy."

Rusty brightened. "You know about billy tea and damper?"

Penny laughed. "Of course I do. Doesn't everyone?"

"Daniel certainly does. He ordered me to have billy tea and damper for our first night out."

"He knows his business."

Rusty tried to think of a way to let Penny know that she didn't have the faintest idea what either item was. No cookbook from Julia Child's to *Joy of Cooking* had recipes for them. It would have been very simple just to ask Daniel, but Daniel was being more obnoxious than usual, due to their sham engagement and marriage. There was no way in the world that Rusty would tell him she didn't know one more thing about Australia. She wondered if she should just take Penny into her confidence. But Penny saved her the trouble.

"Do you know the history of damper?"

"No."

"The word came with the settlers from the British Isles. Damper was something you ate to stave off starvation between meals. It put a damper on your appetite."

"So it means snack."

"Out in the bush the swagmen and settlers called their damper other things. Dorkum or devil-on-the-coals or just plain brownie."

Rusty relaxed. She certainly knew what a brownie was, although she hadn't thought the Australians did. Everything she'd seen resembling American brownies in the bakeries in Adelaide had been labeled chocolate slice, or if it was covered with coconut, a lamington. Evidently here it wasn't called a brownie unless it was eaten outdoors. She wondered if the next mystery could be as easily solved. "How did billy tea get its name?"

"From the billy it's cooked in."

Rusty felt she was getting close to an answer. Daniel had called a big pot with a wire handle and a lid a billy. "I see. If you make tea in a billy, it's billy tea."

"Exactly."

It seemed silly to boil water in a giant pot, then scoop it out into cups with tea bags in them when a teapot would be more efficient, but Rusty nodded as if she understood. She had given up believing she would really understand everything about Oz anyway.

"And of course, a man out in the bush would add a handful of gum-tree leaves to flavor it," Penny continued in her best used-to-be-a-schoolmarm voice.

Rusty made a mental note to pick up plenty of herbal tea bags so they could skip the gum-tree leaves.

"Anyway," Penny continued, "I don't think it's billy tea and damper you should be worrying about. It's all those nights alone with Daniel."

"With Daniel and a dozen passengers," Rusty corrected her.

"Ah, but they won't be sleeping in your tent, will they?"

"Neither will Daniel. He told me he always sleeps outside unless it's pouring down rain. He likes to keep an eye on things."

Penny shook her head at such a furious tempo that Rusty could only catch glimpses of her satisfied smile. "Maybe that's what he's always done, but he's a married man now. Everyone will expect you to sleep together."

"I don't care what they expect. I agreed to pretend to marry him—not to pretend to sleep with him. Let the passengers think what they will." Rusty opened the front door of the Benedicts' house and held it as Penny pushed the pram through.

"You'd better care what at least one passenger thinks," Penny said as the door slammed shut behind her. "Amanda MacCready will be on this trip with you. Anything that doesn't look all-up straight will go right back to her aunt.

And you know what that means.'' Penny drew the side of one finger across her throat in an unmistakable gesture.

"So the Yank drives you to violence, too, does she?" Daniel walked into the hallway, his felt hat in hand.

"Why Daniel, darling, I thought you'd be home sleeping off the excitement of our wedding night." Rusty went to him and straightened the collar of his shirt with wifely efficiency. "Considering everything, though, you're looking fit."

"If we'd had a wedding night, you wouldn't be able to joke about it."

"I don't know. Humor can liven up even the dullest of experiences, don't you think?"

"I will be so glad to see you both leave on your trip! All this sniping. It's awful!" Penny took Julia Rose from the pram and held her over her shoulder. Danny, after a quick hug to Daniel's knees, had already left the room.

"Sniping? Daniel and I are just making conversation, Penny. Old married people's conversation." Rusty pinched Daniel's cheek, moving back quickly enough to keep him from retaliating. "And to think we have two solid weeks together to continue it."

"I came to see if you'd changed your mind." Daniel grabbed Rusty's shoulder and held her still. "It's not too late to back out."

"I think I'll put the baby to bed. You two can finish this without me, can't you? Or do I need to be here to mop up the blood?" Penny waited for an answer, and when none was forthcoming, climbed the stairs with Julia Rose.

"I'm not about to back out," Rusty told Daniel when Penny was gone. "I'm going to see Australia."

"You do realize this isn't going to be a bang-up little picnic."

"I know." Rusty looked at Daniel suspiciously. "What's this all about, anyway? You need me. Why are you offering me this chance to get out of this farce?"

"I've been bashing my brain trying to think of a way to get us both out of it." Daniel flashed his most dazzling grin. "I think I came up with an answer. I'm going to tell Mrs. Mac you left me standing at the altar. She'll be so sympathetic, she'll let me keep my job."

"No way. I'm not playing the heartless hussy—not even to get out of pretending to marry you."

"I heard what Penny was telling you." Daniel's grin had disappeared. "Amanda will be watching us. If you go on this trip, we are going to have to look married. That means sleeping together, cuddling, kissing."

"Spare me the gory details." Rusty lifted her chin and her eyes locked in battle with his. "It will be my most demanding role, but I can handle it. You'd be surprised at the men I've had to pretend to kiss."

"Nothing about you would surprise me."

"Oh, I don't know, Daniel. You might find a few things about me surprising." She lowered her lashes a fraction and gave him one of the smoldering looks that had skyrocketed the sale of Aura shampoo. The air between them seemed to crackle with electricity. She lifted a finger and drew a line from his earlobe to his mouth. "You might even be surprised what can happen to a man who believes there are no surprises in store for him." She moved a little closer, fastening her eyes on his mouth. Very slowly she moistened her lips with the tip of her tongue.

Daniel seemed mesmerized. With her free hand Rusty unbuttoned the top two buttons of her blouse, exposing nothing but promising everything. She moved a little closer while her finger traced a line along Daniel's bottom lip. She bent her head toward his, stopping mere inches away.

"Once I had to stand on a beach with a fierce wind whipping my hair around my shoulders and a dress as thin as a cobweb that parted to expose my leg all the way to here." She took Daniel's hand and rested it on her jean-clad thigh, well above the knee. "The man I was with was gorgeous—a young Cary Grant. I had to put my hands on his shoulders, like this," she demonstrated as she went on, "and bend toward him as the camera zoomed in on us. Then I had to kiss him. Just this way." She covered the inches between them slowly, brushing her lips over his to capture them finally in a kiss that was all show. She moved her head back a little and looked straight into Daniel's eyes. "The man had been eating onions. But the commercial went on to become a classic, Daniel. Kissing you might be a little more difficult, but the result will be the same: a classic performance."

"Do you think so?" Daniel's fingers dug into Rusty's shoulder as she began to pull away from him. "Shall we see?"

"I think we've both seen."

"You've seen nothing." Daniel's other hand brushed over her hip, caressing as it went, until it was pressing against the small of her back. His fingers fanned out until each one separately pressed her toward him. He only stopped when her body fit snugly against his. Then the hand gripping her shoulder smoothed its way along her neck to tangle in the curls at her nape.

"I still haven't seen anything," Rusty murmured, but even to her own ears, the insult didn't quite come off.

"Have some patience, Yank. A good thing can't be hurried. There aren't any cameras rolling here." His lips nuzzled under the curls spilling onto her forehead. They were soft and warm as he drew them down to the space between her eyebrows. His hands edged her closer. He continued kissing her, moving down her nose to stop before he reached her mouth. Then he began on her ear.

"Daniel, this isn't funny." Rusty tried to draw away as the feel of his lips and tongue began to weaken her knees. "We'll call it a draw." The last word came out as a gasp.

The word he breathed in her ear sounded strangely like "surrender." He traced his lips along her chin, avoiding her mouth again, to tantalize her other ear. Rusty tried to squirm away, but her struggles only seemed to bring her closer. "Daniel!"

"More?" Daniel's lips traveled down her neck to her shoulder and along her collarbone. He arched her toward him until his mouth was playing with the soft skin she had uncovered when she'd unbuttoned her blouse.

"Stop it, Daniel!"

His lips on hers choked off the rest of her words. He took advantage of her cry to plunge his tongue into her mouth and begin an exploration that ended, irrevocably, with the cessation of all struggles and the igniting of Rusty's passionate response. Her body seemed to melt into his until no boundaries existed between them.

This was Daniel Marlin. She could not pretend otherwise. But this was a Daniel Marlin she'd never expected to know: Daniel Marlin, desirable lover. And who was she? Certainly not the woman she'd been seconds before. Who was this creature who could lose herself so completely in this man's arms?

He increased the pressure of his mouth, and she yielded. He caressed the side of her neck and she moaned. He matched the softness of her body with the hardness of his own, and she felt as if she'd come home. Everything he did was exactly what she wanted, no more and no less. They had been made for giving pleasure to each other. They had been made for each other.

When Daniel drew away, his eyes opened and held hers. Rusty knew instinctively that what had begun as a game had ended quite differently for him, too.

"If we'd had a wedding night," he said finally. "That's how it would have begun."

"But we didn't have one." Rusty realized her hands were trembling, and she clasped them behind her back so that he wouldn't see. With the end of the kiss her good sense was returning. What had possessed them both? "And we aren't going to have one. And we aren't going to do that anymore," she ended, nodding her head as if the matter were settled.

"Too right." Daniel stepped back a pace and picked up his hat, which had fallen on the floor when he'd embraced her. He jammed the hat on his head, and with its presence he seemed to recover some of his arrogance. "So don't go starting things you don't plan to finish. I'm only human. You and I are going to be packed together as tight as sheep in a shearing shed for the next two weeks."

"You can count on me not to start anything at all. But I'm going with you, Daniel, so get used to the idea."

Daniel tipped his hat and left, closing the door quietly behind him. And Rusty, who had recently sworn to become the soul of honesty, wondered if all along she'd been lying to herself about her reasons for agreeing to the sham marriage in the first place.

The Outback Odysseys Adelaide depot was really nothing more than a small garage where company vehicles were serviced and stored between trips. There was an attached office and a separate storage area for camping supplies. Someone had hung bright travel posters at odd angles on one wall of the office, and the warehouse itself was decorated with a lone yellow sign that read: Last Indoor Dunny for 1,000 Kilometers.

The depot was buzzing with life when Rusty arrived on Monday morning with six plastic bags of groceries strung over her arms. Guides whose names she couldn't even remember hugged her—groceries and all—in congratulations, and Daniel, his face a blank mask, came over to give her a husbandly peck on the cheek.

By far the worst moment arrived right along with Jane MacCready. With sentimental fervor the Iron Maiden broke out a bottle of champagne to celebrate Daniel and Rusty's marriage. Although no one got more than a few drops, the gesture was touching, considering Mrs. Mac-Cready's views on alcohol consumption. Rusty was so choked with guilt she couldn't have swallowed more, anyway.

"If we don't get out of here in a few minutes, I'm going to tell them the truth," Rusty whispered to Daniel. "I've never felt like such a rat."

"Rats desert sinking ships," he whispered back. "Try not to be true to type."

She was spared the necessity of answering. With a few more words of congratulation everyone went back to their jobs, and Rusty and Daniel were left alone to finish packing their vehicle.

The vehicle itself had been an education for Rusty the first time she'd seen it. Built by Mercedes-Benz, it was an all-terrain four-wheel-drive Uni-Mog, large enough to seat eighteen passengers comfortably, and large enough to store all the camping equipment, luggage, fresh water, food and diesel fuel they would need for a safe trip. If she'd had some hazy picture of rundown jeeps plowing through the desert, that picture had been transformed immediately. Now she also understood what a big venture beginning their own company would be for Alan and Daniel. Daniel had explained that equipment of this caliber was not just preferable to have, it was mandatory. The Outback was no place to break down.

Now Rusty watched with interest as Daniel finished sliding canvas tents and plastic mattresses under the luggage locker in the back of the Uni-Mog. She had already stocked the shelves and the cooler box. The groceries she'd spent so much time and energy selecting had looked forlorn and unappetizing sitting there waiting for the trip to begin. She hoped they looked better cooked.

"Come on." Daniel stood and wiped his hands with a rag. "The passengers will start arriving any minute. We should be inside to greet them. You go on, I'll pull the Mog around front."

It was too late to decide not to go, but for a moment Rusty could only stare at him.

"Come on, Rusty. Get a move on." Daniel strode off only to turn around and come back to her when she didn't move. "What is it?" he asked impatiently.

She shook her head, at a complete loss for words. How could she tell him that she had the most momentous feeling that this trip was going to change her life?

"Are you going to back out?" he asked bluntly. "Now's the time, if you are. Once we get going, it will be almost impossible to change your mind."

She shook her head again.

"Then what is it?"

"Do you know I've never slept outside once in my whole life?"

Daniel threw up his hands as if in prayer. "Now she tells me!"

"You never asked."

"Well, you're about to make up for that, Yank. After tonight, you'll never be able to say that again. And after this trip, you'll know what it's like to appreciate that nice cushy life you've been leading." He strode off again and this time he didn't come back.

Rusty watched him go and wondered just exactly what she'd be appreciating in two weeks. At that moment, she couldn't hazard a guess.

Well, you're about to make up for that, Yank, aren't you? . . . you'd never be sad to see that again. And after this trip, you'll know what it's like to appreciate that one thing life you've been lacking." He stared off again and this time he didn't look back.

Rusty watched him go and wondered just exactly what about to appreciating in two weeks. At that moment, she couldn't imagine a thing.

Chapter Six

October 27th

Dear Sly,
New York seems very far away. Did you know there are places in the world where people worry less about what kind of shampoo to use than whether there will be enough water to keep them alive? It makes you think.

Thoughtfully,
Rusty

"It's so vast, so desolate." Rusty stood on the steps of the Uni-Mog and stared at a vista unlike any she'd seen before. The view in front of her went on forever in varying shades of browns and olive greens. It was broken by an occasional mallee tree whose branches rose in stunted patterns like the bent spokes of an umbrella. Instead of grass, clusters of low, scrubby saltbush lay in patches over rock-

strewn red ground. Amazingly, there were a few cattle
grazing on the saltbush, replacing the red-dust-covered
sheep they had seen on better pasture during the earlier part
of the day's journey. Rusty looked down at Daniel and
shook her head. "I never knew the Outback would be like
this or that it'd be this close to the city."

"This isn't the Outback. And if you don't get a move on,
we're going to camp right here instead of up the road where
we're supposed to." Daniel finished filling a pitcher with
fresh water for the passengers to mix with fruit juice cor-
dial, a syrupy nonalcoholic mixture that was an Australian
staple.

Rusty pulled herself back to the mundane chore of rum-
maging through the food storage locker for enough fruit to
serve for afternoon tea. She had discovered in her weeks in
Australia that morning and afternoon tea were sacred
times, and she, too, had quickly fallen into the pattern of
having a midmorning and afternoon snack. Surprisingly,
although she had certainly gained a pound or two, set free
from the restrictions of the diet she'd followed as a model,
her figure had undergone very few changes. Those it had
were for the better.

"What do you mean this isn't the Outback?" Rusty
handed Daniel a sack of oranges and climbed down.

"This is just some dry country. You'll see the differences soon enough."

She wanted to know more, but in the brief hours that she
had been on the road with Daniel she had learned one very
important thing: Daniel was completely dedicated to the
welfare and comfort of his passengers. It had been the force
of his personality alone that had already begun to bind the
group into a cohesive whole. Whatever questions she had
would have to wait until the passengers had been fed and
taken care of.

"Here we go," he announced in a voice that carried to everyone standing in a clump around a creek bed—or what Daniel had called a billabong—fifty yards from where the Mog was parked.

Rusty watched the passengers stroll toward them. She practiced matching names with faces as they came closer. In the front were Perry and Jill Adams, middle-aged American tourists who had only two weeks to spend in Australia and wanted the most intensive experience available during that short time. Right behind them in a cluster were five young women who where traveling together. Rusty knew they were Maureen, Cathy, Annette, Barbara and Luanne, but she still wasn't sure which name belonged to whom. Daniel, of course, had no such problem.

Next there was Peter Collins, an amateur photographer whose equipment looked anything but amateur, and Sally Collins, his wife, who sketched everything that Peter photographed. Behind them came Brock Jennings, a young Englishman in Australia for a vacation, and John Carter, an Adelaide bank teller who had told Rusty he spent all his holidays bird-watching. At the very back of the group, wearing shorts, a provocatively cut T-shirt and high-heeled sandals, was Amanda MacCready.

"They're ace," Daniel said quietly as they approached. "Not a troublemaker in the mob."

Rusty was sure he was right about eleven of the passengers. She was reserving judgment about Amanda.

Once everyone had been served, Rusty leaned against the Mog and ate her orange as she listened to Daniel explain about the cattle property they were on. Daniel knew a lot; she had to give him that. And he had a way of conveying his information that made it easy to forget he was giving a lecture. This was a man she hadn't known existed. As she listened, she wondered what else about Daniel she had missed along the way.

Half asleep in the bright sunshine, she let her mind wander. He certainly looked the part of Outback guide today. He was wearing his white moleskin trousers and an Odyssey T-shirt stretched across his broad shoulders and muscular chest. On his head was the ever-present felt hat tilted at a rakish angle. He'd had his hair cut—she imagined it had been in honor of the beginning of this trip—and he was tanned, brimming with good health, and unbelievably attractive. She had seen the disappointment on the faces of several of the female passengers when she had been introduced as Daniel's wife. If they only knew....

"And as much as I'd like to stay here and tell you more, we're going to push on to Burra, where we'll camp tonight." Daniel wrapped up his lecture and Rusty pulled herself out of her reverie. The passengers climbed into the Mog, but Daniel held her back. "When we get there," he said in the no-nonsense voice he'd begun using exclusively with her since that morning, "I'll teach everyone to set up their tents and the rest of the equipment. You start on dinner. If you could manage without a helper tonight, that would be best."

"I can manage."

He nodded tersely and motioned for her to climb aboard.

They were rattling down a dirt track on their way back to the paved road before Rusty had time to think about Daniel's words. Actually it wasn't his words, but the way he had said them that was worth thinking about. Daniel had assumed an attitude of polite indifference with her that was irritating and intriguing simultaneously. Much hinged on maintaining the pretense that they were married, but Daniel seemed to have abandoned it altogether. He had introduced her as his wife, but not once in the six hours they'd been traveling had Daniel touched her or even pretended to share an intimate moment. She imagined that if his attitude continued, everyone on the trip would begin to wonder exactly what was going on between their guide and cook.

Just why was Daniel treating her this way? Rusty watched him out of the corner of her eye as he drove. She had been surprised to find that her seat was right up front next to his. When the air-conditioning system was turned on and the tape deck blaring as it was now, they could even hold private conversations—if such a thing was ever called for. She wondered just what he would say if she asked him outright what was wrong.

"Well?"

She was startled by his question, but even more so by the tone. He sounded so hostile. Definitely one step beyond disinterested. Evidently something was heating up.

"Well, what?" she inquired coolly.

"Why were you looking at me like that?"

"I wasn't aware I was looking at you. I was admiring the scenery."

His laugh was cynical. "What would a city girl find to admire in a place like this? No shops, no theaters, no beauty parlors."

"Are we going to have a fight?"

He shrugged. "Don't we always?"

Rusty could have pointed out that for a few minutes yesterday they had been as far away from fighting as two people could get. But as that thought occurred to her, so did another one. Daniel's attitude had changed drastically since the kiss they'd shared. As hard as it was to believe, Daniel was upset about something related to that kiss. Now she only had to find out what.

"You know, Daniel," she said carefully, trying to feel her way, "you've been awfully grouchy since yesterday. Not at all like a man on his honeymoon."

His "Humph" sounded as if he'd been taking lessons from Mrs. MacCready.

"If I were a passenger on this tour," she continued, lowering her voice to a near whisper, "I'd have trouble believing you were madly in love."

"Married, not madly in love."

She looked at him to see if he was kidding, but it was obvious he wasn't. "Daniel, they're supposed to be synonymous."

"Bosh."

"Look at Penny and Alan," she said, her voice a challenge. "Two kids already, and they're visibly nuts about each other. And I'll bet when Alan took Penny on his trips after they were married, he didn't go around looking as if he'd like to toss her into the nearest billabong."

"It's a dead cert if I'd tried tossing you in back there, I'd have found out you were a champ swimmer." Daniel turned the steering wheel and the Mog slid onto the paved road. He increased their speed.

It was obvious that he wasn't going to tell her what was wrong. He was too busy trying to start a war. There seemed to be no sense in approaching the situation tactfully; it would be like using a popgun to get an elephant's attention. Rusty crossed her arms and looked straight ahead. "You know, Daniel, if you're afraid that kiss yesterday is going to change anything between us, I can guarantee you that it won't. The kiss was an experiment, that's all. If you slip and forget to be hateful, I promise I won't throw myself at you and plead for another one."

Daniel was quiet for a long time. Then he said softly, "What kiss are you talking about?"

She pulled her arms tighter against her chest as if to keep something inside from spilling out. "Give me a break, Daniel. Give us both a break. I'm on this trip to help Alan and Penny and to see Australia. I'm not after you—as hard as that must be for you to believe."

The rest of the trip was conducted in silence.

Burra was a small town of nineteenth-century stone buildings. Formerly a copper-mining center built by Welsh and Cornish miners, it stood among treeless hills in picturesque isolation. After a quick stop in town to shop and mail postcards, Daniel took them on a tour to see the ruins of the copper mines, the homes tunneled into the side of hills where miners had once lived, and the stone smelting chimneys graced with good-luck statues at the top.

There was excitement in the air as they neared the spot where they would camp for the night. Although most of the passengers were seasoned campers, a few of the women, like Rusty, had never slept outside. Daniel patiently answered questions, gave advice, and made jokes until courage had been instilled and everyone was ready for the challenge.

Everyone except Rusty, that is. She had spent most of the impromptu confidence-building session sinking into a black hole of self-doubt. What was she doing in the Australian Outback with a man who couldn't stand her and a job she didn't know how to do? What was she doing sleeping on the hard ground when she'd never slept on anything harder than the sofa in her living room—and then, only when she wanted to rough it.

When Daniel pulled the Mog onto a grass-covered track that wound between hills, her visions of a nice, clean caravan park disappeared abruptly. The cook, it seemed, was also the official gate opener, and after three trips out to open and close gates, she'd discovered one more important fact: the cook also had to be a mechanic. Each gate was fastened by a different system. When she finished figuring out the last one, her hands, which she still cared for as a good model would, were minus three nicely-shaped finger-nails.

"We won't even make it out of South Australia on this trip if it takes you that long to do the gates," Daniel said when she climbed back in.

In addition to broken fingernails, she knew there was going to be a hole in her bottom lip from chewing it to stop herself from answering him.

They set up camp at the foot of a hill covered by lush green grass. Daniel explained that all the trees in the area had been used to shore up the various copper mines, but Rusty found the stark landscape appealing. Less appealing was the task of making fettuccine Alfredo, green salad, and garlic bread for fourteen people.

Daniel passed back and forth in front of her as she struggled to light the portable gas grill. He passed back and forth as she struggled to fill one of the huge pots with wa-ter from the unfamiliar water system on the side of the Mog. He passed back and forth as she struggled to find the proper equipment and assemble it so that she still had room on the table in front of her. But he stopped, hands thrust in the pockets of his moleskins when he saw what she was preparing.

"Tell me you're kidding."

Rusty looked around to see if there were any passengers near enough to hear them. "Daniel, leave me alone. I'm doing just fine without your cheerful presence."

"Do you know the meaning of the phrase *bush tucker*?"

Rusty nodded. She could feel her temper heating right along with the burner behind her. "'Bush' means out of the city. 'Tucker' means food. In your quaint little Aussie way,

you're trying to tell me you want good country cooking."
She looked up at him and gave a sickeningly sweet smile.
"You shouldn't have married a city girl, then, should
you?"

Daniel looked as if he had something important to say on
the subject, but several passengers were heading their way.
"You'll check the rest of your menus with me," he said
quietly.

"Not unless you want to cook them, too." By now Rusty's eyes were flashing fire. "You got me into this, but you
haven't once thanked me or tried to make this easier. We
have a word for people like you where I come from, Daniel—*insufferable*. I'm not going to take your abuse on this
trip, so butt out. Did you understand that or shall I try to
translate?"

"Daniel, I can't get my pegs in the ground. Will you help
me, please?" Amanda waved her hand from a distant tent
to get Daniel's attention. He turned without another word
and stalked off, leaving Rusty to viciously tear lettuce for
the salad.

Considering that the noodles were overcooked and the
salad too small, dinner was successful, or at least successful enough to be eaten. Afterwards, Jill and the woman
whom Rusty had finally identified as Maureen helped her
wash pots and pans. Since the passengers all washed their
own dishes, cleanup was over in no time.

Daniel had started a small campfire before the meal, and
by the time the washing up was done, the billy had been put
over hot coals to boil. Rusty stood on the sidelines and
watched curiously as Daniel dug a hole and filled it with
more coals. He stood, dusting off his hands when he was
finished and came to her side. "Where's the damper?" he
asked in the no-nonsense voice he'd been using all day.

"I'll get it, and the tea, too."

She returned carrying two large white bags filled with lamingtons and chocolate slice that she'd bought at the bakery that morning. Perhaps if she'd had hours, all the equipment in Penny's kitchen, and several elementary cookbooks, she could have baked her own, but Rusty was nothing if not practical. Making brownies out in the wilds of Australia was definitely beyond her skills.

"What's that?"

"Brownies." She paused. "You know, lamingtons. Damper. You said you wanted damper tonight. Are you going to warm it up in there?" She pointed to the coals.

Daniel's expression didn't change. "What's in the other bag?"

"Tea bags. I got herbal tea mostly, since it's so late and everyone needs a good night's sleep."

Daniel turned back to the fire, squatting beside it. Rusty saw his shoulders shaking. Several of the passengers came up behind them to warm their hands. Surprisingly the temperature had dropped considerably as the sun had gone down. When Daniel finally spoke, his voice was choked. "Rusty, I think you and I need to take a nice, long walk." He stood, and took the bags out of her hands to set them beside the fire. Then, as if he hadn't been biting her head off all day, he took her hand.

They walked between the rows of tents to the sporadic applause of the passengers. Daniel stopped in front of one and reached inside for a flashlight. Then, still holding Rusty's hand, he pulled her along beside him. They had climbed two hills and were on the way up the side of another before he said a word.

"You know, Yank, you're allowed to ask questions."

Rusty was breathing hard. "Am I? Good. Why are we out here in the middle of nowhere climbing hills too steep for mountain goats?"

Daniel stopped and sat down, pulling her with him. When she was settled he dropped her hand, but his comradely manner still lingered. "We're going to talk."

"This trip's going to be full of new experiences."

Daniel turned a little and put his hand under Rusty's chin. "Who told you that the stuff in those bags was damper?" He grinned at her, and as usual, she felt it tug at her insides.

"I figured it out myself." She tried to pull away, but he wouldn't let her.

"You're a stubborn little thing, aren't you? Stubborn and proud and . . ." he paused as if he couldn't think of the right word, "and strong," he said finally. "A very strong woman."

Rusty didn't know what to say.

"Look," he went on, "I know I haven't made this easy for you. None of it's your fault, is it?" He dropped his hand and turned to stare into the darkness. "But from now on, if you're not sure about something, ask me."

"What is it I'm not sure about?" she asked, still confused.

"Damper, for one thing. Damper is dough cooked in the ashes of a fire, or at least in a camp oven. It's what the settlers survived on when they were out in the bush like this, and it's a tradition out here. Most of the time it's just flour and salt and water with leavening or not, depending on what you like."

"Penny told me damper was also called brownie," she said haughtily.

"She put you crook. Sometimes if it was small and cooked in small cakes, they called it brownie, or if they added a little sugar or raisins, they might call it brownie, too. But that stuff you bought isn't damper. You can't buy damper."

Somehow, having Daniel tell her she was proud hadn't been too bad, but being faced with the evidence was a different story. All she'd had to do was admit she didn't know what damper was and ask someone to explain it fully to her. But she hadn't wanted anyone to know she was so ignorant of Australian terms. She hadn't even wanted Penny to know. Maybe Daniel wasn't the only one in this relationship who could be insufferable. She swallowed hard. "Maybe you'd better tell me about billy tea, too."

"It's black tea thrown in a billy of boiling water and steeped. Sometimes we thrown in a handful of gum leaves, too, or stir it with a gum-tree branch. If your spoon melts when you stir it, it's strong enough."

"No herbal tea bags?"

"No tea bags at all."

"You must think I'm a fool."

Daniel was silent for a while. "What I think," he said finally, "is that you and I are going to have a bloody awful two weeks together if something doesn't change."

"Why do you suppose we irritate each other so?"

Daniel didn't answer.

"Will you make the damper?" Rusty asked finally. "I'll watch and then I can do it from now on."

"We'll eat the stuff from the bakery tonight. I'll make damper tomorrow." Daniel stood. "We'd better get back." He held out his hand to help her stand.

Rusty took it, but once she was on her feet, Daniel didn't let it go. "You don't irritate me," he said, pulling her a little closer. "You nibble at me in some odd sort of way. I never feel at peace when you're around."

"You make me sound like some kind of parasite."

Daniel's grip on her hand tightened. "Or some sort of fever."

"Every woman wants to be thought of like that." Rusty tried to pull away, but Daniel's arm came around her.

"I don't want to have another go-in with you."

"You could have fooled me."

"Maybe we're both getting fooled." Daniel's arm tightened around her and then abruptly he let her go. "Follow me back and don't wander. I might want to get rid of you, but not out here."

"I could find my way." The words were out before she realized her stubborn pride had formed them.

Daniel handed her the flashlight, turned and started back over the hill. "Do it then." He paused at the top of the ridge. "You did hear my lecture on snakes this afternoon, didn't you? Just remember, if you seen one, it's probably venomous. But only about fifteen varieties are fatal to humans." He disappeared from sight.

But not for long. Rusty was trotting meekly behind him before he'd gone another twenty yards.

The campsite was humming with activity and laughter when they rejoined the passengers. Someone had made tea in the billy and someone else had passed out the baked goods. Rusty and Daniel sat down to join the conversation. It was only after she'd eaten two lamingtons and drunk as many cups of milk-laden tea that she realized that everyone was trying to smother giggles, especially the young women.

"What did we miss?" Rusty asked finally.

Her question was greeted with peals of laughter. Rusty wondered if all Daniel's trips got off to such a roaring start. This group already seemed like one big family.

Luanne, a chubby young woman Rusty's age, stood and stretched. "Time to go to bed."

As if on cue everyone else stood, stretched and headed for their tents. "Good night, honeymooners," Luanne called, and the others chorused the same as they disappeared through canvas flaps.

Rusty felt her cheeks burn with something other than heat from the campfire. She couldn't look at Daniel. Suddenly the immensity of the lie they were living was all too plain.

"We'd better get to bed, too," Daniel said heavily.

"Where are you sleeping?" Rusty poked the fire with a stick to avoid looking at him.

"With you."

Her gaze locked unwillingly with his.

He held up his hand to stop her from answering. "There's nothing to be done about it."

She knew he was right. Although neither she nor Daniel had mentioned that they were newly married, the word had gotten out to everyone on the trip, probably from Amanda. If she and Daniel didn't at least sleep in the same tent, everyone would wonder why.

"Which one is ours?"

Daniel pointed down the row, and then lowered his finger, turning back to her. "It used to be right there at the end of that row, across from Amanda's." He smiled sheepishly, then bellowed, "All right, mates, where's our tent?"

Laughter echoed off of canvas walls. Luanne poked her head through her tent flap. "Oh, Daniel, Rusty, was that your tent we moved?"

In spite of herself Rusty chuckled.

"Does anyone remember where we put Daniel and Rusty's tent?" Luanne called.

"Not me," everyone chorused in unison.

"A regular mob of jokers." Daniel kicked dirt on the fire, finishing it off with a pail of water. "Let's go find home sweet home, Yank," he said.

Twenty minutes later Daniel held the canvas flap of their tent open and motioned Rusty inside. The passengers had hidden it well in a thicket of bush between two nearby hills. The message had been clear: the honeymooners needed privacy away from everyone else. The passengers had been delighted to give it to them.

If Rusty had believed that she and Daniel could still maintain a modicum of privacy separated by the center pole of their tent, she discovered immediately that she had been wrong. Using rope tied to a sturdy sapling, the center pole had been dispensed with entirely. The tent sagged, but in the middle of it were two of the plastic air mattresses supplied by Outback Odysseys. On top of them were Rusty and Daniel's sleeping bags. Zipped together.

"Well, well." Rusty sat down on the sleeping bags and hugged her knees. "Here's my bed. Where's yours?"

"You're sitting on it." Daniel fastened the mosquito netting around the door and then turned to watch her.

She shook her head slowly. "Daniel, Daniel. You keep forgetting I'm not your type. I'm sure you'd sooner sleep with a rattlesnake."

"We don't have rattlesnakes here. Make that a death adder."

"What a sweet little name for a snake." Rusty stretched and looked around the tent. The passengers had even brought her suitcase in. Suddenly she was very tired. "I have just enough energy to undress and get into my sleeping bag. Now you can help me unzip these and move them apart, or you can sleep on the floor and rough it like the tough Australian man you are. Take your pick." The last words were accompanied by a yawn.

When she opened her eyes Daniel was still watching her. Finally he grinned. "You do crack hardy, don't you?"

"Just what does that mean?"

He shrugged. "You're a right good sport about all this. Most females would be blushing or giggling or simpering...."

"On occasion I blush or giggle, but I have never simpered in my life. I wouldn't know how. I think your view of women has been tainted by all those empty-headed brunettes with vacant eyes."

"Empty-headed brunettes with vacant eyes?"

"Penny's definition of the women you date." Rusty felt along the side of the sleeping bags until she found a zipper.

Daniel knelt beside her and together they separated the two bags. Before Rusty could pull the top one off, however, Daniel covered her hand with his own. "There's nothing vacant about these." He stroked his fingertips around her eyes. "They're always dancing. You're enjoying all this, aren't you, city girl?"

"Everything except digging my own dunny." And trying to cook when she didn't know how, but she didn't add that.

"And sharing a tent with me?"

"Nothing to it."

He drew his fingertip down toward her lips. "I suppose that sharing quarters with a man is old hat for a New York model."

"Did you want a list of names and places?"

Daniel was close enough that Rusty saw something flicker in his eyes at her flippant answer. She almost wished she could call back her words, but then, she didn't owe Daniel any explanations about her love life or lack of it. She didn't owe him anything.

He dropped his hand. "It wouldn't surprise me if you had one."

"Think what you want to, Daniel. We're not really married, remember?" Rusty stood and pulled off the top sleeping bag. She dragged a mattress several feet to the side of the tent and folded the bag lengthwise over it. "If you'll turn off the flashlight, I'd like to get undressed."

"No worries, Yank. I don't want to watch." Daniel flicked the switch on his light and the tent was black except for the faintest traces of moonlight filtering in through the netting.

Rusty undressed, pulling a clean T-shirt out of her suitcase. Then she got into the sleeping bag and zipped it around her. She waited until she'd heard the rasp of Daniel's zipper before she turned over to face him again.

"I may be all the things you hate, but I'm also the woman you're supposed to be married to. You'd better get your act together tomorrow or nobody's going to believe it." As she was drifting off to sleep she wondered why she and Daniel couldn't carry on a normal conversation. Every time they began to get close, one of them did or said something to anger the other. Perhaps there was more to it than she understood at that moment, but one thing was certain: they were oil and water; two people so totally different from each other that they would never be able to share anything except their mutual animosity.

Somehow, it seemed a terrible shame.

Chapter Seven

October 28th

Dear Sly,

Ah, married life! What could be sweeter than waking up next to the one you love?

The picture on the front of this card is a koala. Did you know the males snort like pigs when they are courting? This one reminds me a little of my new husband, warm and cuddly, and since he married me, always up a gum tree.

Romantically,
Rusty

Rusty signed the postcard with a flourish and dropped it into her purse to mail later in the day. She'd been awake for half an hour, ever since dawn had crept through the tent flaps. Her tent mate had no such problem.

Daniel looked like a little boy when he was asleep. Rusty found it hard to believe that the man who tormented her so could ever look so peaceful, so innocent. His brown hair flopped over his forehead to tease his eyebrows; his eyelashes lay in half-moons on his flushed cheeks; the tiny smile on his face was not unlike that of little Danny's right before he stuck his thumb in his mouth.

Of course, there was no question that she was going to be misled by anything as treacherous as Daniel's sweet expression. This was the man who had made her life miserable since the day she'd got off the plane in Adelaide. This was the man who called her "Yank" in a tone that could forever sever all relations between their respective countries. No, this was Daniel Marlin. But wasn't he a beautiful specimen of the human male?

"Do you always examine the men you sleep with like that?" Daniel opened his eyes and stared at her.

Rusty was tempted to tell him the truth—that his was the only face she'd ever seen on a pillow next to hers—but she saw no reason to parade her innocence before him. Let Daniel think what he wanted. Let him wallow in his own prejudice. Knowing Daniel, she was sure he'd find some way to make a joke out of her virginity if she told him.

"Only when the man needs waking up and I'm trying to decide between a slosh of cold water or a kangaroo in his sleeping bag," she answered, turning to find her hairbrush to untangle her hair.

"Don't." Daniel reached over and put his hand on her arm before she could lift the brush to her curls. "Don't comb it yet."

"Why not?" Rusty waited for the joke that was surely coming.

"You have no idea how cute you look." Daniel seemed surprised at his own words, but he followed them up by unzipping his bag and coming over to kneel at her side. Rusty was gratified to find he was wearing nylon jogging shorts, no doubt in deference to her presence in his tent. She wished his chest weren't so bare, so wonderfully, gloriously bare. He touched her hair almost reluctantly. "You should have your picture taken just this way. I'm sure you'd be able to find another modeling job if you did."

"With my hair uncombed and no makeup?" Rusty laughed uneasily. With both of them half undressed and Daniel so close, she felt very vulnerable. No matter what she thought about Daniel Marlin, she couldn't forget what a physically attractive man he was. Nor could she forget Sunday's kiss.

"Too right. Do it, and I'll bet you find work again."

Rusty raised her eyes to his. "It was never a question of finding work, Daniel. I'm not in Australia because I'm unemployed."

He nodded, but his slight smile showed what he was thinking. "Right-o."

"Look, Daniel," Rusty's eyes began to flash amber warning signals and her uneasiness vanished, "I was a very successful model. Very successful. Now you may have trouble believing it's true, but it is. I came to Australia to get away from all that and to figure out what I wanted to do with the next part of my life, not because I couldn't find a job."

Daniel squeezed her shoulder and turned back to his own sleeping bag. "Right-o."

"Right-o, yourself!" Rusty unzipped her sleeping bag and slid out, pulling her T-shirt low over her hips. If Daniel bothered to look, all he would glimpse were two long, shapely legs.

They dressed with their backs to each other, and Daniel was gone before Rusty turned around again. She tried not to think about the fact that they had thirteen more mornings like this to get through. Besides, there was another, more immediate problem to worry about.

Breakfast.

Breakfast for Rusty had always been dry toast and coffee, prepared by Irv, the owner of the deli one block away from her apartment. It wasn't that she couldn't make toast and coffee—that much she could do if she had a toaster and an electric percolator—but eating it at Irv's with a *New York Times* in front of her had been an important tradition.

Out here in the bush there was no Irv. There was no toaster or percolator, in fact there was no electricity. And breakfast on the tour—she'd been informed by both Daniel and Penny—was to be a full-blown meal so that the passengers would feel they were getting their money's worth.

Rusty wondered how many of them would ask for a refund after her efforts had been eaten. She wondered how they would feel about fettuccine Alfredo for breakfast.

If the day hadn't started badly enough, she discovered on arriving at camp that skimpy-playsuit-clad Amanda was to be her kitchen helper for the day. Each of the passengers was to take a turn, and Rusty had hoped that one of the two married women who could surely cook would volunteer first. One look at Amanda's soft white hands and blank expression, and Rusty knew she could count on no real assistance. Breakfast was up to her.

"Can you grill bacon?" Rusty asked the girl, who was staring into space in Daniel's direction.

Amanda shrugged, hardly disturbing the perfect symmetry of her nearly bare shoulders.

"Well, give it a try, will you? I'll get the eggs ready to scramble." Rusty lit the gas grill and got the bacon out, setting it in front of her less-than-helpful helper. "When you're done with the grill, we can make toast on it." At least that's what she'd been told by Penny. Rusty couldn't imagine anyone making toast on the flat metal surface.

Amanda was still staring at Daniel when Rusty came by again carrying egg cartons. "You know, Amanda," she said as calmly as she could, "if we have to serve that bacon raw, some of the other passengers might object."

Amanda looked down at the bacon and then up at Rusty. "Why did Daniel marry you?"

The question had been asked with more irritation than curiosity. Rusty's initial reaction was to tell Amanda in no uncertain terms just where to get off. Then she was struck unexpectedly by a memory. "How old are you?" she asked the girl.

Amanda picked up the bacon and began dropping it on the grill. "Seventeen. I'll be eighteen in July," she added quickly.

Rusty had been seventeen once, too. Seven years before. What a difference seven years could make. There had been a Daniel in Rusty's life then—at seventeen most girls probably had a Daniel in their lives. Hers had been named Trevor. Lord, she had loved Trevor. Like Daniel, he'd been about twenty-eight and gorgeous. Unlike Daniel, he'd been very, very married. He'd also been her piano teacher. Perhaps that was why she'd fallen so hard. At seventeen she had been more immature than most of her friends, completely unready for a serious relationship. Gorgeous, happily married Trevor had been wonderfully safe to love. She had worshiped him from a distance, and now she suspected that if he'd ever come even an inch closer, she would have run like a scared rabbit.

Amanda was more forward than she had been, but Rusty suspected that Amanda's crush on Daniel was very like

Rusty's crush on Trevor had been. Australian girls seemed to lack some of the hard-edged sophistication of their New York counterparts. Amanda was voluptuous, and she worked hard to make herself enticing, but there was a certain innocence about her. Perhaps she had chosen Daniel to love because Daniel, even unmarried, had been one of the most unavailable men around. He, like Trevor, had been safe. Now he was safer still.

Once past Daniel, Amanda would go on to other men— available men. Whatever she learned from this one-sided love affair would hopefully teach her enough to cope with their demands. Rusty felt a surge of affection for the girl poised on the brink of adulthood. Part of being liberated, she decided, was to be secure enough to reach out a hand and help other women through the pitfalls of femininity.

"You'd have to ask Daniel why he married me," she said, putting her hand on Amanda's shoulder. "But I can see you're quite aware of the reasons a woman would marry him."

Amanda looked surprised at Rusty's sympathetic tone. She shrugged the friendly hand off her shoulder and turned to the grill without saying a word. Rusty wasn't offended by her reaction. Amanda had some growing up to do. Perhaps some of it would get done on this trip.

Breakfast was the disaster Rusty had hoped it wouldn't be. The bacon was limp, the eggs stiff and the toast the color of charcoal. She apologized profusely as she served each passenger, wondering just how long she could blame her mistakes on unfamiliarity with the grill. To her credit the coffee was decent, and everyone drank several cups to wash down the ruins of their meal.

Daniel said nothing—an occurrence that worried Rusty more than the insults she'd expected would have. She wondered if he was storing up his comments to add to the ones he'd get to make about dinner that night. As the passengers brought tents to store in the Mog, she washed and packed the grill. By eight o'clock they were ready to depart.

The road to the Flinders Ranges where they were to camp for the next two nights passed through gradually higher hills covered by solid carpets of purple wildflowers. Daniel told them that the flowers were called either salvation Jane or Patterson's curse, depending on whether the speaker was an optimist or a pessimist. Rust-colored sheep stood in the middle of purple fields, and stone cottages, some with thatched roofs, decorated the increasingly lovely landscape. Once they rounded a sharp corner to see three huge birds running in clumsy, flopping strides by the side of the road.

"Ostriches? In Australia?" Rusty snapped a picture through the mud-spattered windshield.

"Emus. Quite different, really."

Rusty wondered if Daniel ever got tired of explaining the same things over and over again. He was never impatient, never condescending, not even when it was Rusty herself asking the questions. She actually found herself looking forward to his sporadic lectures. The accent that had seemed strange to her at first now seemed musical and fluid. Liquid Australiana. The words and phrases that had been confusing now seemed perfectly clear. And Daniel had a wonderful speaking voice, deep and resonant. She wondered if he sang.

Her question was answered about an hour after they ate a lunch of sandwiches and canned salads, neither of which even she could possibly have ruined. Annette was a musician and she deftly organized everyone aboard into a singalong. When they began "Waltzing Matilda," the unofficial Australian national anthem, Daniel joined in. His voice was a mellifluous baritone, and Rusty—who didn't know the words anyway—hummed as softly as she could in order to hear him better.

By the time they arrived at Wilpena Pound in the Flinders Ranges, the group had become even more cohesive.

They set up camp in an official camping area, just a stone's throw from the shower block. The passengers were more enthusiastic about the running water than about the mountain ranges, but once everyone had taken the shower they'd missed the day before, they were ready for an afternoon hike.

"We'll eat later than usual tonight," Daniel told Rusty as everyone got ready to go. "If you're back by half-past five or so there should be time for you to go, too."

"Won't it look strange if my loving husband doesn't come with me?"

Daniel grimaced. "No worries. I'll just tell them I've got to have a bash at a leaky radiator or something."

Rusty and the passengers started down a path that gradually got steeper and steeper. Huge mottled gum trees shaded their way, and once they stopped at a placid stream that a passing hiker told them was ninety feet deep in the middle. After they passed an old, abandoned stone homestead sitting at the foot of the mountains, the group split in two. Rusty and Peter and Sally Collins decided to walk into the center of the Pound, a wide flat area that was rimmed by an almost perfect circle of mountains. The rest of the group opted to climb one of the mountains to a lookout point.

"We'd better turn around about half-past four," Peter said, looking at his watch. "That gives us about an hour to walk in and an hour to get back to camp."

Rusty and the Collinses wandered along a path that took them under giant gums and over vast green fields of waving grass and salvation Jane. Pink wild hops completed the colorful picture, and Peter stopped every few moments to snap photographs.

"Look, Peter," Sally said finally, "we're holding Rusty up anyway, and I'd like to stop and sketch that gum." She pointed to a particularly beautiful specimen of eucalypt. "Let's stop here for a while and let Rusty go on ahead."

Rusty liked the idea. The only problem with the tour was that there was so much time spent driving. She was used to walking distances, although it was usually done on crowded sidewalks, and the idea of stretching her legs at a faster pace was appealing. The path was clearly marked. She would be safe.

"I think I will go ahead," she told the Collinses. "I'll see you back at camp."

The path dipped and climbed gently. Soon she was out of sight of Peter and Sally and on her own. The hot sun was filtered by striated clouds, the air was fresh and sweet, and even the flies, which were a permanent and irritating fact of life in the Australian bush, left her alone.

She had walked a good distance when she stopped to rest and look at her watch. Even though it seemed much later, it was only ten till four. She was reluctant to turn around, but she hated to take a chance on being late for dinner preparations. They would be difficult enough since she'd been told that tonight she had to cook over the fire instead of the grill. While she was trying to decide whether to continue on or head to camp, she looked up and saw a pair of kangaroos looking back at her. They were about fifty yards away, and they were magnificent.

Rusty had seen kangaroos before—in zoos. Seeing them here in the open was a different thing entirely. She felt the same wonder the first settlers must have felt when they discovered these strange, hopping beasts. The kangaroos seemed so tame. She imagined that since Wilpena Pound was a park and no hunting was allowed, the kangaroos had become almost domesticated. She lifted her camera and took a snapshot, wishing they would come closer. Instead they turned and began to spar. She watched in awe as they took playful punches at each other. Standing as quietly as she could she began to move in their direction, snapping pictures as she went. They retreated, she followed. They retreated farther into the bush.

Just as she was about to turn around to find the security of the path, she spotted another kangaroo in a distant clump of trees. Beside it was a joey. Rusty moved in their direction, walking on tiptoe. Even though she was in plain sight, she didn't want to add to their fear of her by making unnecessary noises. As she got closer, the joey did a nose-dive into its mother's pouch, its long back legs kicking the air wildly until it did a flip and was once again upright. Mama kangaroo just stared at Rusty.

She had snapped half-a-dozen pictures and gotten within ten yards of the duo before the mother kangaroo hopped away. Rusty trailed along behind them until she realized she had strayed a considerable distance from the path. She checked her watch. It was still ten till four. She shook her arm and held the watch up to her ear. There was no reassuring tick.

When had the watch stopped working? Before she'd seen the kangaroos? If so it could be much later than she'd thought. She estimated that she had been off the path for fifteen or twenty minutes. If the watch had stopped working right before or after she'd last looked at it, it was probably no later than quarter past four. The problem was that there was no way to tell. She had truly lost track of the time since leaving Peter and Sally. The only thing to do was to begin the walk back and hope she wasn't going to be late.

Wouldn't that give Daniel something to razz her about if she was?

She stepped out of the trees to a small clearing to get her bearings. If she'd been off the path for fifteen minutes she had probably come some distance, although she'd been moving slowly. The sun was no help; she still wasn't convinced that the Australian sun went about its business in the sky the same way it did in New York. If she allowed it to guide her, she might end up in Alice Springs before Daniel and the passengers did.

She lifted her hand to shade her eyes and turned a full circle, scanning the horizon. The trees weren't so dense that she couldn't see around her. In the distance, farther than she would have guessed, she saw what must be the path. All she could really tell was that it was a narrow clearing, rimmed by trees. That was good enough. Nothing else looked familiar.

She started toward the clearing. The grass seemed thicker, but then she'd been concentrating on taking pictures of the kangaroos. She had paid no attention to her surroundings.

Getting off the path had probably not been a good idea. It was the kind of stupid thing Daniel would expect her to do. "New York model lost in Australian bush." Wouldn't Sly love that? If she were found before dehydration or rabid kangaroos or one of Australia's venomous snakes got her, Sly could use the publicity to further her career. He'd find her a job modeling safari wear and sell the story to the *National Enquirer*. "Aura Girl washed hair in Australian billabong while waiting for rescue," she muttered.

It was a good thing she could see the path, or rather, the clearing that she was sure was the path. Daniel would never let her forget it if she got lost. He'd have to come track her as he'd tracked Alan all those years ago. He obviously had the skills. Alan had told her that Daniel had learned to track from an aboriginal man who had worked on his father's station. He could find almost anything or anyone. Daniel's talent had certainly paid off for Alan. Rusty was just glad that she wouldn't have to see evidence of it herself. Daniel was already impossibly conceited.

She realized she was beginning to go up a fairly steep grade. That was strange. She hadn't noticed that she'd been going down when she'd followed the kangaroos. But the clearing was closer now and she made her way toward it. She wasn't going to borrow trouble. The path was right up ahead. And maybe this little knot of fear coiled in her stomach was a good thing. Maybe next time she'd think twice about going off into the bush alone. Maybe she had learned something important.

Unfortunately, it seemed that she still had other important things to learn. "Lesson number two, brought to you courtesy of the Australian wilds," she said out loud, facing the dry creek bed that constituted the clearing she'd hoped was the path. "Never assume that anything is going to turn out right."

Would there be enough time to find the path, get back to camp, and make dinner as if nothing had happened? Rusty realized that she was more worried about what Daniel would think than she was about being lost. Daniel had certainly gotten under her skin. Never, in her entire life, had she cared so much what someone else thought of her. Even when she'd been madly in love with Trevor, she still hadn't practiced the piano any harder. Now she was scurrying around in the wilderness like a kangaroo pursued by a wild dog just because she was afraid Daniel would make fun of her when she finally got back to camp.

She wondered if climbing a gum tree would help her to see far enough to find her way. It seemed like a very sensible idea. She was certainly up a gum tree in every other way. She looked around for a likely candidate. All the nearby trees had trunks so large her arms wouldn't reach around them and branches that began many feet above her head. Across the creek bed she saw a smaller tree, with limbs she could just about touch. She picked her way across, using stepping-stones because although dry, the bed was spongy and not too trustworthy.

She was definitely at a disadvantage, having been raised in a city. She had never climbed a tree in her life. Still, there was always a first time. She'd certainly spent most of her life in buildings that made this tree look like a midget. With a jump, she grasped the lowest sturdy-looking branch and began to scrabble up the smooth bark of the trunk. She'd never been prouder of herself than she was the moment she was able to swing her leg over the branch and begin to propel herself even higher. She was halfway up the tree before she stopped. Her view was excellent. The mountains encircling her were fully visible. She could watch undisturbed as the sun continued to sink behind them. The only thing she could not see was the path.

Rusty began to climb higher, congratulating herself that she wasn't afraid of heights. It was a good thing, really. She was very high now. High enough to see for miles. High enough to injure herself seriously if she fell. High enough to... She shut her eyes and clung to the trunk of the tree like the koala on Sly's postcard. What was she doing up a tree? Was this any way for a successful model to deport herself? Was this any way for a woman alone to explore the bush? Was this any way for Rusty Ames, terror-stricken city girl, to find her way back to civilization?

She had no idea how long she clung to the trunk of the tree, but when she finally opened her eyes, the sun had definitely sunk another notch. It was getting very late. Soon it would be dark. By now people would begin to wonder where she was, if they hadn't already. If the Collinses were back at camp, they would probably tell Daniel where she had headed. Rusty wondered how long it would take Daniel to find her. She imagined that neither Daniel nor all the fabulous aborigine trackers in Australia had ever had to track a redheaded Yank up a tree.

It was her pride, finally—not fear of spending the night alone—that made her begin the climb down. She clung to the trunk, but she risked feeling for the branch below with her left foot. She shifted her weight cautiously, and soon she was sitting on the next branch, then the next. As she prepared to slide the final distance to the ground, she realized she was not alone.

"See anything up there?"

Rusty gazed down at Daniel with a mixture of joy and loathing. "How'd you find me so quickly?"

"You left a trail a blind man could have read. Coming down? Or does it seem like home now?"

"More like home than sharing a tent with you does." Rusty looked at the ground. It still seemed very far away.

Daniel grinned at her discomfiture. "Want some help?"

"Of course I don't!" Rusty regarded the ground once more. Obviously the tree had grown since she climbed it. Gum trees must grow at the speed of light. The good earth was much farther away than it had been.

"Swing around to the branch beside you. I'm coming up."

There was no time to think about Daniel's words. Before Rusty knew what was happening, Daniel was sitting where she had just been and she was comfortably ensconced on a nearby branch.

"Kookaburra sits in the old gum tree, merry, merry, king of the bush is he..." Daniel sang melodiously.

"Cut it, Daniel!"

He swung around to face her. "Did you know there's only one kookaburra in Wilpena Pound? He's fifty-six years old. He was one of two brought here when he was just a fledgling to start a flock in these mountains." Daniel made a raucous laughing noise. Then he listened carefully. The birdcall wasn't returned. "He must not be around here tonight."

"What happened to the other one?"

"I don't know. But I'm sure the one that's left misses his mate. I thought I was going to miss my mate tonight."

Rusty tried to pretend that she and Daniel weren't sitting in a tree having this conversation. "I would have found my way back eventually."

"Tell me how you were going to do it."

"Well, I climbed this tree so I could find the path. I got off the path when . . ."

"When you followed the kangaroos. Two of them, weren't there? And another one farther away, with a joey, I reckon."

"How did you know?"

"Once you realized you weren't sure where you were, you got out from the cover of the trees and turned in a circle to see if you could find your way. You probably spotted the creek bed, thought it was the path, and headed in that direction. Once there, you realized your mistake and decided to climb this tree."

"Amazing."

Daniel shrugged. "So what were you going to do next?"

"Well, I couldn't find the path from up here. So I decided that once I got back down to the ground, I'd follow the creek bed. I hoped it would eventually run into the stream that flows near the campground." She paused. "Would I have made it?"

"Someday. What would you have done for water?"

Rusty shook her head. "Gone thirsty, I guess."

"Let me show you something you should know if you're going to go wandering off like this again." Daniel reached for Rusty's hand as if they were the best of friends. "Hold on to this branch," he put her hand on the sturdy branch right above them, "and let your feet dangle over here." He pointed away from her. "I'll catch you." He swung himself down. Rusty did as she'd been told, and Daniel caught her before she had a moment to get scared. "There now," he said, when she was absorbing the joys of solid ground again. He took her hand once more and started toward the creek bed.

"You recognized this for what it was," he continued, kneeling on a rock. "What you didn't think about was this." Daniel took a stick and began to dig a hole. About six inches down, Rusty could see that the hole was becoming increasingly muddy.

"There's water there," she said, fascinated. "I didn't realize."

Daniel stood, wiping his hands on his jeans. "If you live out here, the first thing you have to know to survive is how to recognize the signs of water. This trick saved my life once."

"Daniel, I'm sorry." Rusty reached out impulsively and put her hand on his arm. "I know I never should have gone off the path. It was foolish and citified." She dropped her hand. "I never would have apologized, but you've been so sweet since you found me. Thank you for not giving me a lecture. And thank you for tracking me."

"What kind of man would leave his darling wife out in the bush? Besides, I was getting hungry. I couldn't lose my cook."

Rusty wanted to tell him that he might be hungry after dinner, too. Daniel was so mellow, he might understand if she confessed that she couldn't cook. After that day's breakfast, he probably wouldn't even be surprised. "Daniel," she began.

"No worries. I was just kidding. Jill got a work crew together to make the meal while I came to find you."

Rusty clamped her lips shut. Her confession could wait. Why spoil such a nice moment? "I guess we'd better get back then, so we can eat it."

Daniel stepped forward and touched her hair. Bending, he planted a lazy kiss on her forehead. "I'm glad you're all right, Yank. I had a few bad moments worrying about you." Before she could answer, he turned and began to make his way through the grass in a direction Rusty never would have taken. She followed close behind—content, for once, just to do what Daniel wanted.

Chapter Eight

October 30th

Dear Sly,
I think I'm beginning to understand Australia, if such
a thing is possible. It's the cheerful bustle of Sydney,
the gracious warmth of Adelaide, the craggy, wild-
flower-covered majesty of the Flinders Ranges. It's
also the endless, lonely, barren stretches of land called
the Outback. Strangely enough, I think I like that part
best of all. With so little to see, Sly, I find I can see so
much more.

Philosophically,
Rusty

"Who do you write all those postcards to?" Daniel
turned his head slightly, his eyes flashing to Rusty's lap for
a second before, once again, he trained them on the empty
road in front of him.

"A man in New York." As soon as the words were out, Rusty wondered why she had said them quite that way.

"Someone special?"

"Sly's special, yes." What was making her continue this game? Why hadn't she told him the whole truth, as she'd told Penny when Penny had asked the same question. Rusty chastised herself for trying to mislead Daniel while another internal voice reminded her that Daniel had no right to ask questions, anyway.

"How does he feel about this trip?"

"He hates the idea. He wants me back there."

"Well, it's a dead bird he'll have his wish when this trip's done."

Rusty wondered if she was imagining the thread of anger in Daniel's voice. "Is it? I don't recall telling you I was heading back right away."

"What would keep you here?"

Rusty didn't answer. Her feelings were too difficult to put into words. Instead, she changed the subject. "Are we almost there?"

"There? Look around. Does it look like there's a 'there' anywhere in sight?"

Actually, it looked as if nothing would ever be in sight again. They were traveling down the Oodnadatta track, interminable miles of dirt road cutting through a desert of sand and salt flats on their way to Lake Eyre, a giant salt lake that more often than not, was almost dry. Daniel had told them that Oodnadatta meant blossom of the mulga. Rusty marveled at the optimism that had moved someone to name the track anything so sentimentally poetic.

"Are we going to just pull over to the side of the road and camp? Or do you have a special place in mind?"

"There's a site I like on the shore of the lake."

"A campground?" she asked hopefully.

Daniel laughed. "Who'd put a campground in the back of beyond?"

"I thought the back of beyond was where people liked to camp."

"Have you seen any people?"

Rusty had to admit the road had been eerily empty. The last town they had passed through, William Creek, had been officially populated by two stalwart citizens. "If there was a quarter as many people as there are flies, this place would be a metropolis."

"Nobody made you come."

Rusty was surprised by Daniel's sarcastic tone. And she was surprised by the hurt she felt at it. "If I sounded like I was being critical, I'm sorry," she said stiffly. "The flies are annoying, and the heat can be bad sometimes, but I wouldn't have traded this chance for anything." She turned to look out the side window. Strangely enough the sun shining through the windshield was making her eyes sting with unexpected tears.

"Why not?" Daniel's tone had lightened a little.

"I like it. All of it."

Daniel was silent so long, Rusty was certain their attempt at conversation had ended. Then he said softly, "I'm fair surprised we have that in common."

Rusty wanted to tell him that the more she was with him, the more she believed they had other things in common. But she couldn't say anything that sentimental to Daniel Marlin. After his unexpectedly mellow mood on the day he'd rescued her from her perch in the gum tree, he'd crawled back into the shell that was obviously meant to keep her at a safe distance. He criticized, teased, or gave her orders, but that was the extent of their communication.

Sometimes she wondered whether, if she'd first presented herself to Daniel as the glamorous Russet Ames, he'd be treating her any differently now. Daniel liked glamorous women. He probably would have been dazzled by her designer clothes, perfectly made-up milk-white complexion, and her beautiful cascading hair. There was nothing dazzling about her now. He had said it best: She was cute. The Australian sun was multiplying her freckles until she actually had hope that someday they would merge into the semblance of a tan. Her hair was a chaotic tumble of curls that even Aura shampoo and conditioner couldn't have tamed. And her clothes? She looked down at her Outback Odysseys shirt and khaki shorts and grimaced.

Daniel began a spiel over the Mog's microphone when they neared their destination. As he talked about artesian basins, land and water levels, and car races in the middle of a dry lake, Rusty continued her fantasy. She ought to shock Daniel into noticing her when they got back to Adelaide. She ought to wheedle him into taking her somewhere fancy and wear the one slinky, designer dress she'd brought to Australia—if it still fit. She could manage something with her hair. And she still knew how to apply the right kind of cosmetics to make herself appealing to a man.

But why did it suddenly matter to her what Daniel thought? He was simply Daniel Marlin, pain-in-the-neck, unliberated, thoroughly uncivilized Daniel.

"Come on, Rusty. Rattle your dags."

They were off the road, but she'd been too involved in her own thoughts to notice. They had arrived—in the middle of nowhere.

"We'll set up camp. Tea tonight should be about six." Daniel waited for Rusty to get up and push her seat forward so he and the passengers could get out.

Tea. Dinner. The evening meal. Rusty tried out all the titles as she climbed down and went around to the side of the Mog to begin setting up the camp kitchen. There was a strong wind blowing across the lake-that-wasn't, carrying with it the tang of salt and a chill that would fast become icy as the sun set. She was too worried about dinner to give it more than a passing thought.

On the night she'd been lost, the passengers had cooked and the meal had been scrumptious. Her mouth watered just to think of it. The next day she had cooked, or rather, she had tried to cook. Fortunately, Sally Collins had been her helper that day, and at breakfast, after watching Rusty spill a half cup of salt into the bowl of broken eggs that already had pieces of shell floating on top of them, she had gently taken over, directing Rusty's efforts so that the meals that day hadn't been bad at all.

Breakfast this morning had been a different story. Rusty had gamely tried to make pancakes. Neither she nor Barbara, her helper, had known what they were doing. The pancakes had been burned around the edges and raw in the middle. Daniel's reaction had been to open three boxes of cereal, which were emptied immediately. And now it was time for dinner. Rusty wondered how much longer she could keep her secret.

"You don't know much about cooking, do you?" Barbara asked pleasantly as she came over to help Rusty.

"Pretty obvious, huh?" Rusty imagined her face was as miserable as her tone of voice.

"Does Daniel know?"

Rusty shrugged. "He's trying to eat the same meals as everyone else."

"Maybe he thinks it's just the grill, like you keep telling us."

"Apparently you didn't believe it."

"No, but I was here watching you cook this morning."

"A sorry sight, I know."

Barbara laughed. "I've got an idea. Sally and I talked about it this morning after brekkie. She and Jill and Brock are all good cooks, and some of the others might be, too. They're going to take turns supervising meals. That way, Daniel won't know you can't cook."

"I couldn't ask them to do that." Despite the miserable feeling of knowing she'd been caught red-handed, Rusty laughed a little, too.

"It doesn't matter. Maybe you'll learn right away. Besides, we'd all like some decent tucker. Here comes Jill, now."

"Rusty," Jill said loudly enough for Daniel to hear, "I enjoyed cooking so much the other day, I wondered if you needed another helper. I'll do whatever you say." And then Jill single-handedly took over the preparation of the meal, assigning only the most mundane tasks to Rusty and Barbara.

When the steaks came sizzling off the grill accompanied by tender baked potatoes and vegetables done to perfection, Rusty watched the expression on Daniel's face. The small deception seemed worth any of the discomfort it was causing her. Daniel was amazed. And after the meal he was obviously a man well pleased with life.

"I didn't know you had a meal like that in you," he told her that night as they prepared for bed.

There was nothing she could say that wouldn't incriminate her or compound the lie—not even a simple thank-you.

She heard the rustling noises of Daniel shedding his clothes over the howling of the wind outside their tent. It was dark enough that they both had complete privacy, but there was something about the sound of cloth rasping against skin that was unbelievably provocative. Rusty wondered what it would really be like if she and Daniel were married. What would come next? Her sleeping bag or his? What would it feel like to sleep entwined with him all night long?

"Do you have to be so noisy?"

Startled, Rusty turned in Daniel's direction. "Noisy?"

"Noisy. Can't you get undressed quietly like I do?"

"You're not quiet. I can hear every piece of clothing come off and hit the floor." Rusty hurriedly finished undressing and pulled on a fleecy track suit. The temperature had dropped enough to need it and more.

"You're doing it on purpose."

"What's wrong, Daniel, darling?" Rusty knew she was provoking him, but she couldn't stop herself. "Feeling a bit frustrated? Such a sad state for a man on his honeymoon."

"You're out of your mind."

"No worries, mate. I understand perfectly," she said consolingly.

"Stop yabbering. I'm whacked and it's early doors tomorrow."

Rusty wondered how she could ever have had trouble understanding Daniel's vocabulary. Everything he said seemed perfectly plain now. She was talking too much, he was exhausted, and both of them had to get up at dawn. "I'm whacked, too. And I'm not yabbering. I'm just pointing out what's going on here. You're irritated because I'm a female and I'm not crawling all over you. You're not used to such a thing. Maybe it would help if you just thought of it as a chance to build your character. Good night, darling. Ooof!" Rusty's words were followed by an exhalation that drove every bit of oxygen out of her body. Daniel's face was inches from hers and his body was stretched across her, pinning her down.

"Nice of you to warm me up," she said, stopping momentarily to fight for air, "but I do have a sleeping bag." She tried to push him away, contacting the cuddly warmth of a sweatshirt, but he took her hands and held them against the ground.

"I'm fed up to the back teeth with your ear-bashing."

"So you thought you'd try a few strong-arm tactics."

"No. I thought I'd educate you a bit about character."

The kiss that followed Daniel's words was surprisingly gentle. He held her hands as he kissed her, but he didn't hurt her, although Rusty imagined he was angry enough to. She had pushed him too far. Had she been trying to provoke him to do just this?

She turned her head to escape the kiss that was rapidly getting out of control. "Get off me, Daniel."

He released her hands to bury his fingers in her hair and turn her head back to his. "Your educating's not over yet."

She remembered another day's education. "Be sensible. This isn't going to make things any easier between us. I'm sorry I got so pushy." She moaned a little as his mouth came down on hers again. Her hands came up to shove him away, and instead they wrapped around his back to bring him closer. She was rapidly forgetting all the reasons why this was such a bad idea.

He knew exactly how fast to increase her pleasure. His tongue stroked her lips just as she was ready for it, he encouraged her to open her mouth just at the moment she wanted the kiss to deepen. His hand traveled down her neck to rest on her breast at the exact second she yearned for it to. He began to move his palm in lazy circles. Rusty could feel her whole body tense with desire. Somewhere deep inside her she felt a warm rush of sensation. How could Daniel arouse her so quickly and so thoroughly? She shifted so her body cradled him completely.

This time Daniel moaned a little. "Who's the teacher here, Yank?" He lifted himself a little and began to inch down the zipper of her track suit. His mouth trailed kisses along the skin he exposed. Rusty threaded her fingers through his hair, but whether it was to encourage him or halt his progress, she wasn't sure.

"Daniel! Daniel!" Shrieks from outside battled with the wind, which by now was rattling the walls of their tent in primitive rhythms.

Daniel rolled to one side and sat up. Rusty could see the outline of his hand silhouetted against the tent door as he pushed his hair off his forehead in a classic gesture of frustration. "I'm coming," he shouted as he stood. "I reckon someone's tent blew over. Probably Amanda's. She's the only person on the trip who wouldn't just get out and fix it herself."

The wind picked up velocity, and for a long moment it was the only sound to be heard. "I'll be asleep when you get back," Rusty said finally, pulling herself together. "Don't forget which side of the tent your bag is on."

She watched as he turned to face her. "You're a passionate little thing. About as passionate as you are stubborn. Too bad about this wind."

"Go fix Amanda's tent, Daniel. Go sleep in it, too. I don't care."

"No?"

Without being able to see Daniel's face, Rusty knew he was grinning. She slid between the edges of her sleeping bag and closed the zipper with one hard yank. "No!"

But she did care. And when an hour had passed and Daniel still hadn't returned, she had to admit that the wind wasn't the only thing keeping her awake.

* * *

The town of Oodnadatta was in as poor repair as the track that bore its name. Originally a stop for the Ghan, the railway that ran between Adelaide and Alice Springs, Oodnadatta had been abandoned by the railroad when the tracks had been moved to a different location. But there had been as many reasons for Oodnadatta to continue as there had been for it to die. The town hung on, maintaining a surprisingly pleasant general store and a drive-in theater consisting of a vacant lot with a pint-size screen and no on-site projector. Most of all, Rusty appreciated the sense of humor that had moved some of the town's inhabitants to give the town a cheerfully obscene nickname and then capitalize on it by selling equally obscene T-shirts to the few tourists who crossed the town limits. The spirit of free enterprise was alive and well in the Outback.

Back in the Mog, Rusty tried to ignore Daniel as she'd been able to ignore him all morning. They were heading to the homestead of a cattle station, the same one where Daniel and Alan had worked years before, and the passengers were buzzing with excitement. There were subtle changes in the scenery. They passed coolibah trees and rocky red sandhills. Daniel had told them they were traveling through Sturt's Stony Desert, and that the rocks covering the ground were called gibber. The endless, subtle variations of the landscape intrigued Rusty, and she found after a time that she could forget Daniel's presence beside her entirely.

"I didn't get much sleep last night. How about you?" Daniel asked cheerfully.

So much for forgetting Daniel. Rusty's cheerful tone matched his. "I slept like a log. I didn't even hear you come back in."

"That's because I didn't."

"Really? You must be tired."

"Tents were falling like calves at a muster. I finally slept in here so I could keep my eye on everything without disturbing you. That was a bonza wind."

Rusty was surprised that the day suddenly seemed much brighter, even though the desert sun had been shining relentlessly since dawn.

She wasn't sure what she'd expected, but when they finally got to the Carter Creek station, Rusty realized how little she really knew about life in the never-never of rural Australia. The homestead complex was almost as large as the town of Oodnadatta had been. The homestead itself was built in the style of many early Australian station houses. It was made of stone with a corrugated iron roof and had a wide veranda on all four sides to offer access to any breeze that might blow by. The yard immediately around the house was green and fenced in by a white picket fence that would have looked perfectly proper surrounding an English country garden. The yard stopped at the fence limits, however, replaced immediately by stone and sand and low, brown scrub.

The other buildings were less picturesque, but tidy just the same. One, built of plywood and corrugated iron, looked large enough to house a family. Another, built of the same materials, had a wooden sign that designated it as the store. Smaller huts rimmed the complex, and behind them were a half-dozen trailers. Two shacks without walls housed well-tended machinery, and in the distance was a low-slung building with a large corral in front of it. A dozen horses, tails swishing, stood in the shade of wind-twisted trees at the edge of the corral.

Daniel had hardly turned off the Mog's engine when a pretty blonde, her long hair flying behind her, ran out of the main house.

"Daniel!"

Rusty moved so that Daniel could make a quick exit. She watched as he leaped to the ground and swung the young woman around, then kissed her. Acutely aware that the passengers were watching, Rusty joined him on the ground.

"Rusty, come meet Melly Symons. Melly, this is Rusty..." He paused for half a second, and then recovered. "Rusty Marlin. My wife."

"Wife? Wife!" Melly grabbed Rusty and kissed her on both cheeks. "I thought I'd be a grandmother without seeing Daniel Marlin married. You poor girl. You'll have to tell me what you did to deserve this larrikin."

"I haven't figured it out myself."

"You're American! That explains it." She winked at Rusty. "Obviously, word about Daniel never reached the U.S."

"Melly's father, Jack, is the station boss," Daniel explained to Rusty. "I knew her when she was all knobby knees and pigtails."

"He still thinks I have knobby knees and pigtails," Melly said, making a cheerfully awful face, "but that's okay. Not everyone is blind to my charms."

"What she's trying to say is that every stockman for two thousand kilometers has proposed to her."

"Every one but the right one. I'm still as single as can be."

As passengers filed out of the Mog, Daniel introduced Melly, who ushered them all inside for afternoon tea.

As a welcome break, Outback Odysseys had arranged for the passengers to eat their dinner and the next day's breakfast at the homestead. Real beds were also being provided in some of the outlying buildings, which turned out to be bunkhouses. Most important, showers were available, too.

Rusty came out of her shower, toweling her hair dry. She entered one of the two bunkhouses that had been allotted to the women to find Jill staring at her.

"Suddenly, you look so familiar," Jill said. "I just know I've seen you somewhere before."

Rusty was sure she knew exactly where Jill had seen her. Unlike the Australians, Jill, whose home was in Minnesota, had to have been exposed to Aura's aggressive marketing campaign. Rusty wanted to giggle. What a strange job modeling was. In her case she was most familiar to the public when she was dripping wet. She had friends whose hands or feet were worth thousands of dollars, but whose faces would never be recognized by anyone.

"I've never been to Minnesota," she told Jill as she pulled on clean shorts and a blouse. "Have you spent time in New York?"

Jill shook her head and narrowed her eyes as if she were trying to see Rusty in a different light. "I know I've seen you somewhere. It'll come to me."

"Rusty looks like Huckleberry Finn." Amanda sat on the top bunk of one of the sets of beds, filing her nails.

Rusty was surprised by two things. One was that Amanda even knew who Huckleberry Finn was, and two, that the girl was capable of saying something so catty. Evidently Amanda was in more pain than Rusty had guessed. Daniel's marriage was a personal betrayal, and Rusty was the cause.

"Guess I'll have to roll up the knees of all my jeans and find a straw hat," Rusty said lightly.

"I'd like to sketch you," Sally Collins said, interrupting whatever Amanda had been about to say. "But not because you look like Huckleberry Finn; because you have the most interesting face I've seen in a long time. Peter's noticed it, too. He's been taking tons of photographs of you. Did you know?''

Rusty was so used to the clicking of a camera, she hadn't even noticed.

"Rusty?'' Melly stood in the doorway. "We've got a surprise for you. Get your suitcase.''

Rusty had a feeling of foreboding. "I'm already unpacked.''

"You'll have to pack up again then. You and Daniel are sleeping in the big house.''

Rusty knew it was too much to hope that she and Daniel would have separate rooms.

"If Rusty doesn't want to go, I'll be glad to take her place,'' Amanda said. "Who knows? Daniel might be glad, too.''

"You're not my kid, Amanda,'' Jill said into the resulting silence, "but if you were, I'd turn you over my knee, even if you are almost a woman. Let's hear an apology.''

Once more the little room was deadly quiet.

"I'm not at all sorry,'' Amanda said finally, although her cheeks were bright red. Obviously she knew she had gone too far. "It's as plain as the nose on my face that Daniel doesn't love Rusty. Their marriage is a joke.''

Melly drew in her breath sharply, but Rusty held up her hand to silence her. "Amanda, you're welcome to think what you like, but next time you want to start a fight, I'd appreciate it if you wouldn't drag the other passengers into it. They came here to have a good time. You might want to ask yourself why you came.'' Rusty bent over and cleared her things off one of the bottom bunks, stacking them neatly in her suitcase. "Lead the way, Melly.''

Inside the house, Rusty realized she was still shaking. Amanda had gotten remarkably close to the truth, and yet it had still hurt to hear it. Daniel didn't love her. Their marriage was worse than a joke: it was a lie. More and more people were being pulled into the web she and Daniel had woven, and in the end, more people were going to feel betrayed. The passengers, Mrs. MacCready, the guides and their wives, Melly. Before it was over with, who else would be hurt by their deceit?

"Amanda has a crush on Daniel. That's why she said those things. I know. I was in love with him too, once upon a time. Of course, I was only fourteen, and it passed like a flash." Melly touched Rusty's arm. "Don't let it bother you."

Rusty smiled. "Thanks, Melly."

Later, sitting on the big four-poster bed that she and Daniel would share that night, Rusty wondered if it was possible to feel more miserable than she already did. Nothing was going as she'd expected it.

And nothing continued to.

Daniel arrived moments later with the suitcase and with an expression on his face that Rusty was sure mirrored her own.

He threw his suitcase on a chair and unsnapped the locks. "We're going riding. You'll need to put on some jeans."

Rusty decided that at least one question had been settled in her mind. It was possible to feel more miserable. "Correction," she said heavily. "You're going riding. I'm going to sleep since I probably won't get much tonight."

"And just how do you think I plan to keep you awake?"

She ignored his question. "Besides, I don't ride. Never have, anyway."

"You can learn, city girl. Everybody's expecting you, and they're all waiting." Daniel went to the door and threw it open. "Bring a hat, the sun's still high. And wear a long-sleeved shirt."

"I've been dressing myself since I was four." Rusty unsnapped the lock on her suitcase and began to sort through her clothes.

"You haven't been dressing for these conditions."

"You got me into this, but that doesn't mean you have to take care of me. Go away." When she looked up, Daniel was gone. Rusty pulled out heavy jeans and grimaced at them. She couldn't imagine wearing denim in this heat. Neither could she imagine wearing a long-sleeved shirt as Daniel had ordered her. Instead, she settled on cotton pants and a colorful tank top, dabbing her arms and shoulders with sunscreen to compensate. She settled a tinted plastic visor over her curls. She might be miserable, but she was at least going to be stylish about it.

Besides, if she were lucky, the trail ride would be short. If she were even luckier, they would run out of horses before she got to the corral. And if she were luckiest of all, Daniel would ride off into the glorious Outback sunset and forget to find his way back.

No matter how miserable she was, there was always hope.

Chapter Nine

October 31st

Dear Sly,

I've been thinking. If any jobs come up for a model demonstrating sunburn remedies, you might think about using me. But please don't consider me for anything on horseback.

Painfully,
Rusty

"That New York bloke must be right important to you if you have to write him in the middle of the night!" Daniel turned over in the four-poster bed and put his pillow over his head to block out the light from the small lamp at the desk where Rusty was sitting.

Rusty wanted to tell Daniel to mind his own business; she wanted to tell him that she liked to stay up this late. But all she could do was make a strangled noise that was more expressive than anything she could have said, anyway.

She had badly underestimated the Australian sun. She had badly underestimated Australian horses and saddles. There was no part of her exterior or posterior that felt normal. She was either burned to a crisp or black-and-blue. And choosing one form of torture over the other would be impossible. She couldn't remember feeling so miserable.

On arriving back at the homestead from the infamous trail ride, Rusty had rushed inside to change her clothes, covering her sunburned skin immediately with the long-sleeved shirt she should have worn while on the horse. She had creamed her face and applied a foundation with sunscreen in it, but her efforts had only hidden the effects of the ride from everyone else. It was not a magic cure to take precautions after the damage was done. Now she was paying for her stubbornness and her pride. And Daniel was the last person she wanted to know about it.

Daniel sat up and threw his pillow down beside him. "Come to bed and turn off that light! I'm not going to jump on you the minute you hit the mattress."

Rusty turned to examine him. His hair was rumpled, cheeks flushed, blue eyes wide and sleepy. Her eyes traveled down to his bare chest, tanned and muscled from the vigorous life he led. He was a dangerous man to share a bed with. A giggle rumbled deep inside her. No man was dangerous tonight. If Daniel came within an inch of her sunburned skin, she'd scream loud enough to wake everyone on Carter Creek station.

"Are you all right?" Daniel narrowed his eyes, then he swung his legs over the side of the bed.

"Don't get up. I'm fine. I'll be in bed a little later. I'll just turn off the light so it doesn't bother you and write post-cards without it.'' Rusty snapped off the lamp, and the room was plunged into darkness.

"Turn that light back on."

"Don't worry about it, Daniel. I can see just fine. I have eyes like an owl's."

She didn't hear footsteps, but before the last word was out of her mouth, Daniel was standing beside her and the lamp was on once more.

Daniel gently turned her face toward the light, shaking his head as he did. "Stay here. I'll be back in a minute." He paused at the door. "How much of you is as red as your face?"

Rusty sighed. "More than you'll ever see. What the sun didn't get the horse did." She waited in misery as his foot-steps retreated. Minutes later she heard him coming back.

"If you'd told me earlier, I could have saved you from feeling so crook." Daniel shut the bedroom door behind him. "Lie down and let me take care of you."

"I can do it."

"No, you can't." Daniel motioned to the bed.

There were times for arguments, times to defend rights, times to take stands. Rusty knew that now was not the time for any of them. If she'd listened to Daniel in the first place, she wouldn't be in this predicament now. Meekly, she did as she was told.

At the bed, she paused. "I don't think I can lie down. It hurts too much."

Daniel made a clucking noise that was surprisingly sym-pathetic. "I should have guessed, after the way you dressed today."

"I know. You told me to be careful, but I thought you were just being patronizing."

"Me?"

Rusty sat gingerly on the bed. "Could you get my back first?"

"Take off your shirt and let's see the damage."

Rusty hesitated. "Um, is that necessary? Couldn't you just lift it or something?"

"You're wearing a bra under it, aren't you?"

She nodded.

"Then take off the shirt so I can see what I'm doing, please." He touched her hair lightly. "Aren't you used to being seen without some of your clothes?"

"Now just a minute!"

Daniel's laughter rumbled through the room. "I was talking about your modeling jobs."

All the fight went out of Rusty. "Oh." She began to unbutton her shirt. "Mostly I was seen wet, wrapped in a towel. My shoulders were bare and my legs." Gingerly she peeled off the shirt until she was clad in nothing except a lacy bra. Stalwartly she reminded herself that it hid more than many a bikini.

"You have lovely shoulders. Lovely pink shoulders."

Rusty imagined that Daniel must be shaking his head. She hadn't looked at him since she'd undressed. "Can you do anything about them?"

"Let's give it a bash."

Rusty decided that Daniel's answer wasn't supposed to be taken literally, because in the next instant he was smoothing something cool and soothing over her shoulders. His hands were infinitely gentle. Rusty suspected she was purring.

"You know, Daniel," she said, to keep her mind off the feel of his hands sliding over her skin, "you're the only person I've ever known who could have provoked me into doing something this dumb. Why do you suppose we react to each other the way we do?"

"So now the sunburn's my fault?"

"No. What I mean is that if anyone else had suggested I dress a certain way, I wouldn't have thought twice about doing it. You tell me to do something and immediately I do just the opposite."

Daniel began smoothing the ointment over her arms, but he didn't answer.

"Well?"

Daniel finished her arms and came around to kneel at her feet. He raised his hands to her face, and then to her neck, making slow, gentle strokes. Then he slid down to her chest and the valley between her breasts. He lingered there, running his thumbs under the rim of lace in a movement that seemed more provocative than thorough. "You really want to know? Fair dinkum?" he asked when he'd finished.

"Yes. Fair dinkum." Rusty realized she was breathing unevenly.

"You're falling in love with me."

Rusty knew her jaw dropped, but only for a second. She gasped, choked, and then gave into the inevitable. She fell back on the bed in helpless laughter. "Ouch! Daniel!" Rolling to her side she tried to smother her hysteria in the pillow. "I must have gotten sunstroke, too. You won't believe what I thought you just said."

Daniel took advantage of her helplessness to unsnap her pants and begin to pull them off.

"What are you doing?"

"I brought some liniment, too. We'll have you as good as new."

"I don't want to be as good as new. Stop!" Rusty laughed again and kicked at him, but Daniel ignored her halfhearted attempt to stop him and finished stripping off the pants.

"Look at you," he said severely. "Your legs are raw. This stuff would sting like crazy. I'd better use the ointment."

"I'll do it." Rusty sat up, holding him off with an outstretched hand. "Lord, Daniel, if I'm so madly in love with you, I might ravish you if you do it." She giggled, but this time the sound was distinctly tremulous.

"I've considered that. It seems worth the chance."

She giggled again, but it was the last time. There was something in Daniel's eyes that stilled her laughter. She held out her hand for the ointment, but Daniel shook his head. Kneeling again, he pulled her toward him and began to smooth the ointment on the chafed spots between her legs.

"No more." Rusty tried to pull away, but Daniel held her still.

"I'll be done in a flash." His hands made light circular motions, caressing the supersensitive skin between her thighs.

She clamped her jaw shut, forcing herself to endure the bittersweet intimacy of his fingers. She had brought this on herself, but Daniel's gentle stroking was more punishment than she deserved. Finally he straightened and began to replace the cap on the ointment jar. "That'll do."

"It feels better." Rusty wondered why she didn't feel better, too. Her insides were in a turmoil. She wanted to ask Daniel to hold her. She wanted to feel the coolness of his skin against her entire body. She felt vulnerable, and sensitive, and scared.

Daniel stood. "Maybe we can both get some sleep, now."

Rusty sat up and pulled the sheet down. With her back to Daniel she stripped off her bra and put on the biggest T-shirt she owned. In a moment she had gently lowered herself into a comfortable position on the bed, leaving plenty of room for Daniel. She forced herself to sound normal.

"Thanks for your help. I'm sorry you had to rescue me again."

"No worries." Daniel turned off the light. Rusty felt the bed sag under his weight. Then she felt his arm come around her. She caught her breath in protest, but his kiss was as gentle as his hands had been. "This arrangement is a bit too tempting. That sunburn might be a lucky thing for us both," he said softly, his lips against her ear.

"It might be at that," she admitted.

"You might ravish me after all."

"At times you're a very ravishable man."

He hesitated before he answered. "If I was ever at the mercy of a woman, Yank, I'd like it to be you."

She touched his cheek. "So would I." She touched his lips. "I'd be gentle with you, Daniel."

"I believe you would be." He kissed her finger, then her lips. "But if the shoe's ever on the other foot, don't expect the same from me." He turned over and moved to his own side of the bed. "Good night."

"Good night." Rusty listened to his breathing, waiting for it to slow and even out with the onset of sleep. If it ever did, it was hours later, after she had finally fallen asleep herself.

Ayers Rock rose out of the deep red of the desert like a Precambrian monolith. Rusty understood immediately why the aboriginal people considered it a sacred place. It lay on a flat plain surrounded by spinifex grass and mulga scrub, and it kept watch over the surrounding desert like a benevolent monarch. Rusty had seen larger mountains, she had seen snow-capped peaks and fir-tree-covered slopes, but never had she seen any mountain that held the impact of this one. It was easy to believe that Uluru, the Loritdja tribal name for Ayers Rock, was truly the heart of the great Australian continent.

"She's really the weathered peak of a buried sandstone ridge," Daniel told the passengers as they neared the base of the Rock. "You'll see her change colors tonight, and if you get up early enough tomorrow, you'll see her change colors then. She can go from the deepest violet to the brightest orange."

"It's beautiful. Oh, Daniel, it's so beautiful." Rusty touched his arm. "And to think I might have missed it."

He smiled at her, turning quickly back to the road. "I'm glad you didn't."

In the distance, about forty kilometers away, another group of mountains rose from the desert floor. Daniel explained that Katajuta, the place of many heads, or the Olgas, as the mountains had been called by the first Europeans to discover them, were not made of sandstone like the Rock, but of a boulder conglomerate. They would visit both, walking through some of the Olgas' gorges and climbing to the top of Ayers Rock. For most of the passengers, this stop was their main reason for choosing the tour.

Rusty listened as Daniel recounted some of the Dreamtime legends of the aborigines who had inhabited the area. Each formation had its own meaning, its own story, its own place in the creation of life. Daniel knew them all.

Daniel's respect for the original Australian inhabitants and their descendants was just one of the things that Rusty had grown to appreciate about him. He was one with his country, experiencing it on the many levels it offered. He was at home here among myth and legend and the hot desert sun. He was at home in the unique world of cattle stations and equally at home in the city. Rusty had watched him take the passengers from one experience to another with an ease that she couldn't help but admire. He was self-possessed in a way that no man she'd ever known had been. Daniel didn't see life as a challenge nor did he see it as something to be gotten through. Life, for Daniel, was something to wade into slowly; to savor, to experience, to drift with when necessary.

The night before, camping in the middle of nowhere, Rusty had found Daniel beside the campfire staring into the flames that he had gone to extinguish. She had squatted beside him, watching the flames, too. "Daniel," she had said, aware that it might be the first serious thing she had ever asked him, "what is it you see there?"

"Nothing and everything." He had reached out for her hand, and they had squatted there in companionable silence with the Northern Territory desert wind blowing through the sandhills around them. "It's all there, Rusty," he had said finally, standing and pulling her up beside him. "Did you see it?"

Somehow, she had understood. She had nodded silently and he had kissed her, as if to share the intensity of the moment in the only way he could.

She had followed him back to their tent, and he had moved his sleeping bag close to hers, falling asleep with her hand held securely in his. Rusty had lain awake wondering why everything seemed different between them since the night at Carter Creek station. They still argued. She still reacted unreasonably when he told her what to do; he still teased her unmercifully. But the edge was gone—softened by the sun perhaps, softened by the Outback winds. Daniel had become real to her, a person with needs and desires and the formless, nameless yearnings that had led him into this country and moved him to show others what he saw. He was no longer her tormentor. At least not in the same way.

She was quite aware that her attraction to him was growing right along with her understanding. She saw clearly now what it was about Daniel that drew women to him. It wasn't his grin and his broad-shouldered physique. It wasn't eyes as blue as the Outback sky. It was something else—something intangible and rare; a certain presence that made Rusty feel safe with him. Safe and alive and happy. Strangely enough, being with Daniel did make her happy now. And that was certainly something to think about.

She listened as Daniel finished their tour of the base of the Rock. He pulled the Mog off to the side of the road beside a cluster of mulga trees, and she handed out paper bags with lunches in them that the passengers had put together that morning. When all had been distributed Rusty sat on the ground, leaning gingerly against a tree. But by now her sunburn was really only a bad memory; Daniel's ointment and loving attention had helped immeasurably.

As she ate her sandwich she watched Amanda follow Daniel to another tree and plop down like a faithful puppy dog beside him. Since her confrontation with Amanda at Carter Creek, Rusty had seen an escalation in the girl's attempts to get Daniel's attention. Amanda was rarely more than a few feet from Daniel now. Rusty expected to find Amanda sleeping in their tent soon if the campaign continued.

Daniel treated the girl's obvious admiration for him gently and with humor. He never complained, and he didn't tease her the way he teased Rusty. Best of all, however, he never encouraged her. He was polite, and he was kind. Both were more than Amanda deserved.

"Does that bother you?" Jill sat next to Rusty and pulled out her sandwich. "If it was Perry she was after I'd scratch out her eyes."

Rusty smiled. "Sure, it bothers me. But it would bother me more if Daniel responded to it."

"He's very good with her, really. Someday she'll look back on this and see how foolish she was. At least she won't have to remember Daniel's scorn."

Rusty tried to remember Jill's words that afternoon as the passengers hiked through the Olgas and Amanda hung on to Daniel's arm. She tried to remember Jill's words that night when the entire group went to a pub at the nearby Yulara Tourist Resort and Amanda begged Daniel to dance with her most of the evening. She tried to remember them when dawn arrived the next morning and Amanda came to their tent door to ask Daniel to show her the best place to see the sunrise over the Rock.

Finally, she tried to remember those words after breakfast when Amanda attached herself to Daniel and insisted that he help her climb the Rock. By then, however, Jill's words were only a whisper. The one thing Rusty could remember was that Amanda was a pain in the neck.

"I'm sorry, Amanda," Rusty said, coming to Daniel's side. "But Daniel's promised me his help today. I know John or Brock will be glad to help if you need assistance."

"Daniel's job is to help the passengers." Amanda's eyes were narrow slits.

"My job does not include helping passengers hike up the Rock," Daniel told Amanda before Rusty could say another word. "The hike is your own decision. If you don't feel strong enough to make it, don't go."

Amanda's eyes widened, and Rusty saw they were filled with tears. "I'll just go by myself!" She whirled and ran after a small group of the passengers who had gone on ahead.

"I shouldn't have said anything," Rusty said heavily. "I shouldn't have intervened. It's not like you're really my husband."

"And if I were?"

Rusty remembered something else Jill had said. "I'd scratch out her eyes." She made a face. "No, really, Amanda's just so head over heels in love with you she doesn't know what she's doing. It's so hard to be that age."

"Says the wise old woman." Daniel put his hand under Rusty's chin and lifted it. They stared at each other until he finally dropped his hand and turned away. "We'd better go if we're going to climb."

"I just said that to keep Amanda away from you. I hadn't really planned to try it." Rusty looked at the steep, smooth red rock without so much as a bush on its surface to hold on to. The summit was 348 meters above the surrounding plain, and to Rusty's eyes it looked as if the designated walking path went straight up. A low chain fastened in the rock stretched up the middle of it, but the beginning and the end of the climb would have to be under her own power. To a city girl used to elevators and sidewalks, it looked impossible.

"We're going. You have to do it, Yank."

"Why?"

Daniel shrugged. "To say you have."

"Not nearly a good enough reason."

"Then you have to do it because I'm going to drag you all the way up and back if you don't."

Rusty shut her eyes. "Do you remember the day I was up the gum tree?"

"Could I ever forget?"

"I couldn't get down because I was afraid."

"Were you afraid going up?"

She shook her head.

"Then, no worries. You'll get up fine, and once we're there, you can sit down, I'll give you a fair-size push and you can slide all the way back to the ground."

Rusty opened her eyes to see Daniel's gorgeous grin. "You would too. All right, I'm going. But I'll get myself down."

"Good on ya." Daniel draped his arm over her shoulders and they started toward the Rock.

With Daniel behind her, Rusty began the climb. Enough people had died trying to reach the summit of Ayers Rock for the climb to be treated with caution. Daniel had told them the rules that morning. Don't stray off the path, don't take any unnecessary chances, and don't push yourself too hard. Now Rusty added her own rule: Don't look down. She knew Daniel was right there below her, but she only knew it by his cheerful urgings.

"We're past chicken rock now."

Rusty was panting. "Chicken rock?"

"Back there. You're not looking."

"You're right. I'm not. If I look, you'll have to put me on your back and carry me the rest of the way."

By the time she reached the chain, Rusty's knees were shaking from the exertion. She sat down, grasping the chain, and looked below her. "Good Lord." She shut her eyes immediately. "How are we going to get back down?"

"First you've got to worry about getting up." Daniel climbed a few feet above her and sat down, spreading his legs around her so she could lean against him. He put one arm around her waist. "Did you know you hair's the color of the Rock at sunset?" He rested his cheek against her curls.

"Don't tell my agent. He'll want to use this place in one of my commercials."

"What kind of commercials?"

"Shampoo and that sort of thing." Rusty decided to change the subject. "Do you realize we're cuddling like old married people?"

"Um."

"It's nice not to be fighting, isn't it?"

"Very nice."

Rusty liked the sound of his answer and the feel of his cheek against her hair. "I could get used to this, you know. I've always thought I'd get married someday, but I never realized just how nice it would be to always have the same someone to share moments like this with. I like the idea of building memories, exploring together, growing old together."

"Mates."

"The best kind of mates. I guess this crazy scheme has taught me something after all." Suddenly it seemed important to know if Daniel felt the same way. "You told me once that getting married wasn't in the cards for you. After this, do you still feel that way?"

"Is this a proposal?"

She laughed and gently poked her elbow in the firm flesh of his abdomen. "Come on, Daniel."

"There aren't many women who could live with me."

"So you admit you're difficult."

His arms tightened around her. "Look out there in front of you. That's my life."

Rusty stared at the endless miles of Outback scenery. "If a woman loved you, Daniel, she'd find a way to fit herself into your life. And there is such a thing as compromise."

"I couldn't ask any woman to share this. It's no life for a woman."

"Alan and the other guides manage. I think you're hopelessly—" she started to say chauvinistic, but changed it "—old-fashioned."

"I would never ask a woman to give up an easy life for a hard one. I'm out here twice as much as Alan and the others are. Know anyone who'd want to put up with that?"

"If this hypothetical woman was someone like me, she'd convince you she wanted to be with you, whatever that meant. She'd find a way to make it good for both of you."

"Whoever she is, she sounds like a match for your bloke with the halo. Getting all starry-eyed and hoping for the best doesn't mean a thing."

"But caring enough about someone to believe that any problem has a solution does mean something. It means everything."

Rusty could feel Daniel's sigh. "Besides," she continued, "I think you sadly underrate the country that you love so much right along with women in general. This is a wonderful place. Men have no monopoly on loving the Outback. Melly Symons told me that she wouldn't live anywhere else."

"I'm not in love with Melly."

The message seemed so clear that at first Rusty wondered if she was imagining what she'd heard. Was Daniel in love with someone? Could it possibly be... "Who do you love?" she asked, and her voice was husky.

"I didn't say I loved anyone." His voice was husky, too.

"If you did, she'd be very lucky."

"And here I thought you'd be itching to tell her your views on Aussie men."

"I'd give her a gentle, well-meaning lecture, right along with my congratulations."

A group of four hikers passed them, followed closely by another group.

"We'd better get going," Daniel said. Rusty felt him stand behind her. She slid around on her bottom to view the rest of the climb. Reluctantly she took Daniel's hand and stood, too. They had been so close to something—some revelation just under the surface. She felt cheated.

The chain had been placed on the steepest portion of the Rock, and Rusty knew that without it, she never would have made the climb. When the chain ended, the slope leveled a little, but the climb was still difficult. She was grateful for Daniel's hand. They were almost to the summit before they noticed a knot of people clustered on the other side of a narrow natural bridge they had to cross to reach the summit.

"What's the problem?" Daniel quickened his pace, dragging Rusty behind him.

"Daniel!"

Rusty saw that most of the people were passengers from their tour group. She felt a twist of fear at the expression on their faces. "What's wrong?"

They were over the bridge before Rusty had time to worry about the steep drop-off on each side. Daniel dropped her hand and hurried over to the crowd, and Rusty followed right behind him.

Amanda was lying on a narrow ledge seven feet below the path. Her face was a deathly white and her eyes were closed.

"What happened?" Daniel knelt beside the drop-off.

"She was showing off." Perry Adams stepped forward. "If she hadn't fallen just where she did, she would have become one of those statistics you told us about. Brock, here, grabbed her just as she was about to go over the side headfirst. She darn near took them both down. He managed to swing her to that ledge before he lost his grip on her.

Daniel's face was grim. "Amanda, can you hear me?"

Amanda opened her eyes. Even from a distance Rusty could see how frightened she was.

"Daniel, I'm scared to move."

"Don't move. Just stay right where you are. We'll get you back up."

"I'll bet her ankle's sprained pretty badly," Brock said. "She landed on it when I dropped her, but I doubt anything else is really wrong. She's just shook up."

"Are you all right?" Daniel asked him.

"I will be after another night at the pub."

Rusty couldn't imagine how they were going to get Amanda back up. The ledge was the only one for yards, and it was more of a brief outcropping in the smooth red rock than a bona fide ledge. There was little extra room for anyone to stand. She was just leaning over to offer the girl encouragement when she felt a hand snake around her waist and jerk her backward.

"What the blazes are you trying to do, Rusty?"

Rusty realized this might be the first time that Daniel had actually used her name. She wasn't "Yank" or "city girl."

"I was just going to try and talk to her."

"Do you think I want to lose you down there?" Daniel spun her around, and Rusty saw that his face was pale. Before she could comment she'd been wrapped tightly in his arms. He held her against him as he made plans with the passengers for a rescue.

Minutes later someone else held her as she watched Daniel go over the side to get Amanda. She had pleaded with him not to do it, to wait for the rescue team that Cathy had gone for, but Daniel had been afraid that Amanda's fear might cause her to do something more foolish than she had already done. As his face disappeared and then his hands, she realized she was no longer breathing.

"He's going to be all right. He's got the belts to hold on to." Jill tried to soothe Rusty.

"What if they don't hold?" Rusty had watched the men hook their belts together in lieu of rope. The plan was for

Daniel to slide down to the ledge to Amanda. Then he was to hook the makeshift lifeline around her and boost her up. The men at the top would do the rest, then send the belts back down for Daniel.

"All the belts are made out of sturdy leather. Daniel won't put any more stress on them than he has to."

Rusty stared wide-eyed at the spot where she'd last seen Daniel. When the top of Amanda's head appeared, she tried to move to the edge to check on him, but Jill held her back. It was only when Daniel was standing in front of her himself that she realized her cheeks were wet. The tender look on his face when he realized she'd been crying was all she needed to throw herself into his arms once again.

"I didn't know you cared, Yank," he said, for her ears only.

"Just hold me a minute, would you?"

He did until she'd calmed down a little. Then, with obvious regret, he set her away from him and went to Amanda's side. "Amanda, can you open your eyes?"

The girl was still and white. None of the ministrations of any of the other passengers had brought a response, but at Daniel's words Amanda's eyelids fluttered open. She groaned. "My leg hurts."

Rusty could see that the girl's ankle was already beginning to swell. Despite herself, Rusty felt sorry for her.

"What's the best way to get her down?" she asked Daniel.

"We're going to have to let the rescue team come up here and take her down on a stretcher. They're trained to do it."

Amanda groaned again and shut her eyes.

In less than thirty minutes the rescue team arrived with their stretcher and skillfully loaded Amanda on it. Rusty and Daniel waited until the team was halfway down before making the climb back themselves. The passengers had elected to stay at the summit and unwind.

Concern for Amanda kept Rusty's mind off the steep hike, and they were at the bottom before she realized she should have been scared to death.

"Nothing broken," one of the rescue-team paramedics told Daniel, when he and Rusty approached, "but you'd better have it x-rayed in Alice just in case I've missed something. It is badly sprained. She's not going to be doing any hiking for a while."

"How do you feel, Amanda?" Daniel knelt beside the girl and examined her expertly bound ankle.

Amanda turned her face away from him, but not before Rusty saw the gleam of tears.

"You know you'll have to go home now, don't you? There's an airport here. We can have you back in Adelaide tonight, and your own doctor can take care of this."

Rusty reached down and put her hand on Daniel's shoulder. "If it's not broken, Daniel . . ."

He stood, shaking his head. "We've got a tour to run. Amanda's going to need more care than anyone here can give her. I can't take the time, not with the other passengers to see to."

"I'll do it." Rusty looked at the pretty teenager and then back at Daniel. "I can do it easily. And the others will help."

Daniel looked at her strangely. "Why would you want to?"

"I was seventeen once."

"Not so long ago." Daniel touched the tip of her nose affectionately before he turned back to Amanda. "Well?" Daniel's voice carried the question.

"I want to stay." Amanda's voice seemed to come from far away.

"You'll have to do what Rusty tells you to. And you'll have to go into Alice and have a doctor look at your ankle."

"I will."

Daniel smiled a little. "Then I guess I'll leave you two alone to work out the details."

Rusty waited until Daniel was too far away to hear her. "Well, I guess the only thing we really have to work out is how to make you the most comfortable. Can you put any weight on the ankle at all?"

"I've made such a fool of myself." Amanda turned to Rusty, and tears were streaming down her face. "Why do you want to help me? It's your husband I'm in love with."

Rusty sighed and sat down beside her. "It's because of Trevor."

"Trevor?"

"Trevor was my 'Daniel' when I was seventeen. I remember just exactly how it felt to be in love with someone who wasn't in love with me. You might think nobody understands, but I do."

Amanda sniffed and her lip trembled. "I'll always love Daniel."

"I believe you. I still love Trevor even though he's got four kids now, and he's half bald. When I see him, my heart skips a beat or two. But the difference is that now I can giggle at my own reaction. Someday you'll be able to giggle at the way you feel about Daniel."

"But you've got Daniel to help you forget about Trevor!"

"And someday some man is going to help you forget Daniel."

Amanda sniffed again, but her lip had steadied. "When did you realize Daniel was more important to you than Trevor?"

"Well, there were some men in between. I dated a lot, just like you will, and I fell in and out of love about a dozen times. Then Daniel came along and I saw just how incredibly different he was, and I knew . . ." Rusty's voice trailed off. What was she saying? And why was it coming straight from her heart? There was no deceit. This was not one of the string of lies she and Daniel had been caught up in.

Amanda seemed not to notice Rusty's silence. "I hope that happens to me someday," she said wistfully, "because I know Daniel isn't going to fall in love with me now. He's got you. He loves you. At first I didn't think he did, but I've been watching him lately, and now I know I don't have a chance."

Rusty didn't know what to say. Her own words were ringing in her ears. She patted Amanda's shoulder instead. "I see the paramedic left you a crutch. If I help you stand, can you use it to get to the Mog? Or shall I get Daniel to carry you?"

"I'd like to have Daniel carry me. But I guess I'd better walk. Will you help if I need it?"

"That's what women are supposed to do for each other."

"Then I'm glad I'm just about a woman."

Amanda held out her hand and with Rusty's help she stood.

Chapter Ten

November 4th

Dear Sly,

A goanna, just like the one on this card, visited our camp today. Her frightful lizard exterior hid the soul of a cover girl. Our goanna posed for pictures with the patience of a pro, then took the eggs we offered her and scurried away. I'm living in a land where people are outnumbered by kangaroos and rabbits, outsmarted by magpies and ring-tailed possums, and outshone by cockatoos and parrots. Who said that humans are the superior species?

Humbly,
Rusty

Rusty dropped Sly's postcard in the slot of the post office at the Yulara tourist resort. After making Amanda comfortable, she'd completed the odds and ends of shopping she'd needed to do for that night's supper, and she'd bought herself a souvenir sweatshirt. Now, the little snack bar with outdoor tables beckoned. After all, she was on vacation. The visions of sugarplums dancing in her head could become reality, just as long as she realized that she'd have to slim down again when she got back to New York— if she ever got back to New York. Today, immediate gratification seemed more important than pandering to an uncertain future.

"I'll have a chocolate malted shake, extra thick." Rusty drummed her fingers on the counter in anticipation.

Outside at a shady table she sipped her milk shake and watched people dart in and out of the various shops. She waved to Peter and Sally Collins as they came out of one, carrying a small package. "Come join me."

Sally collapsed in a chair beside Rusty and waved to disturb the small swarm of flies that were visiting, too. Daniel had told them that the casual swat was called the Australian salute, and in the ten days they'd been on the road, it had become instinctual for everyone.

"I want lemonade," Sally told Peter who went in to order for them. "I love the bush," Sally told Rusty, "but this little bit of civilization in the middle of it's a treat."

"It looks like you've been shopping."

Sally accepted her lemonade from her husband and waited until he was seated, too. "Not shopping. Peter got his films developed. He couldn't wait to see what he had."

Peter opened his package and began to sort through the photographs, passing them around the table as he finished with each one. "Here's one of you, Rusty, and here's another."

Rusty, who was more accustomed to seeing her image on film than most people, made the appropriate complimentary noises.

"I had a feeling you'd photograph well," Sally told her. "Have you ever thought about modeling?"

"Actually, I used to do some." She pointed at her milk shake. "Too many more of these and I'll have to model circus tents."

"May we join you?" Jill and Perry came across the square, and Peter pulled up another chair. "Pictures?" Jill asked. "May we see?"

Jill and Perry oohed and aahed over the photographs, but Jill stopped short when she saw a particularly striking one of Rusty in front of a ghost gum. "I know I've said this before, but you look so darned familiar, Rusty."

Rusty slurped the last few drops of her milk shake and pushed her chair out from the table. "Well, if I don't get back soon, dinner's going to be late." Sally stood, too, but Rusty waved her back to her seat. "Thanks, but I'm going to do this one with Luanne tonight, Sally. Daniel's getting suspicious with so many extra people clustered around the kitchen. Luanne promised me she knows how to grill lamb chops, and I'm sure even I can't mess up mashed potatoes."

"I think you're improving," Jill said, still gazing at the photo of Rusty. "Last time I helped you, I hardly had to say anything."

"Well, you did have to remind me to snap the green beans."

"She was going to boil them ends and all," Jill explained to the others. "But you never will again, will you?"

"We'll see. We're having them for dinner again tonight."

Rusty walked along the path that led back to the campsite. It was surprising, really, how intimate the tour group had become. Being together day in and day out, they'd developed a special camaraderie, and even though the trip had four more days to go, people were already exchanging addresses. A romance had even developed. John, the quiet Adelaide bird-watcher, and Maureen, a Melbourne sports enthusiast, were spending all their time together.

Rusty looked up from the path to see Daniel coming toward her. She switched her bags to one hand and waved. "You didn't have to come after me. I was just going back to start dinner."

Daniel waited to answer until he was beside her. "Actually, I did come to find you." He lifted several of the shopping bags from her arms and turned back toward camp. "You missed sunset at the Rock last night because you were cooking. Since we're eating earlier tonight, would you like to see it?" He paused and cleared his throat. "Just you and me?"

Rusty wanted to find a quip to lighten the atmosphere, which suddenly seemed laden with something she didn't understand. Nothing came to mind, however, except "Yes, I'd like that."

"I think most of the passengers have plans for the evening. We won't be missed."

Rusty felt the stirrings of guilt. "What about Amanda?"

"Cathy is staying to play cards with her."

"That doesn't seem fair."

"Cathy doesn't seem too worried about it."

Dinner was surprisingly good. Rusty wondered if she really was learning to cook. True, Luanne had done the hardest part, but she, herself, had managed the potatoes and beans without burning or oversalting them. Even dessert was a success, although Rusty had to admit that ruining canned pudding would have been difficult for anyone.

She showered quickly afterward and changed into the nicest casual clothes she had brought with her. The forest-green slacks and green-and-rust flecked shirt set off the bright tones of her hair and the amber of her eyes. She had combed her hair twice before she realized that she was taking as much care with her appearance as a woman going out on a special date.

A date with Daniel. She fluffed her hair with her fingers and left the shower block. Daniel was just being kind; this was no date, not really. He was showing her the same consideration he would have shown any of the passengers who had missed the sunset. Perhaps he was even trying to pay her back a little for coming on the trip to help him keep his job. It was true that only a little more than a week had passed since they had left Adelaide, but the intensity of their time spent together had broken down both their defenses. Since they were no longer fighting all the time, Daniel probably felt comfortable enough with her to be nice now. But this certainly wasn't a date—nothing like it.

"Ready?"

Rusty looked up to see Daniel coming out of their tent. He had changed, too. He was dressed in slacks and a light blue shirt, and there was no hat on his head. Rusty suddenly felt unbearably shy. "I'm just about ready. Let me get my camera."

The Mog seemed empty with only the two of them inside. When Daniel spoke the sound filled it. "There's a place I know where we can watch the sunset away from everybody else. Are you game? Or would you rather stay with the mob?"

Rusty wondered if she was imagining the challenge in Daniel's voice. "Let's go to your place." She laughed a little. "Isn't that what they always say in old movies when someone's about to be seduced?"

"If I seduce you, it won't be on a sandhill."

"Whew. I'm relieved to hear that."

"It'll be somewhere more private. Like our tent."

She laughed nervously. "Our tent's not private. I can hear Barbara and Maureen turn over at night. And Perry snores—or Jill does. I'm not sure which."

"When we get back, we'll find our tent all by itself like we did the first night. I heard a bit of plotting."

"Oh." Rusty wondered why her heart seemed firmly attached to her vocal cords. "Daniel," she said cautiously, "I'm not much on seductions. Despite your prejudices about big-city models, I think you've got the wrong girl."

"No worries. I know which girl I've got."

As they neared the Rock, Rusty tried to figure out exactly what he'd meant.

One of the beauties of Uluru National Park was that there were no campgrounds or hotels within twenty kilometers of the Rock itself. They had all been located at Yulara so that the Rock could be appreciated for its beauty without distractions. Now Daniel bypassed the tourist buses that had brought their passengers to view the spectacular sunset effect and turned down a bush track. He pulled off after a few minutes and parked.

"We'll have to walk a ways."

"It's a go." Rusty smiled at Daniel. "How was that?"

"There's nothing for it. You're turning into an Aussie." He brushed the back of his fingers over her cheek.

"Then I'm a bit of all right?"

"A real beaut."

"A bonza sheila."

"We're going to be late." Daniel pinched her cheek.

Outside the Mog they walked hand in hand along a footpath that led to a clump of desert oak trees. The day had been a scorcher, but as it usually did in central Australia, the air was quickly chilling with night's approach.

"This is as good a place as any." Daniel stopped and pulled Rusty to sit beside him on a large rock jutting out of the center of the trees. The trees made a half circle behind them, shielding them from the path, but their view of Ayers Rock was unobstructed.

"You should take your first picture now," Daniel instructed her. "Then you can take them at seven- or eight-minute intervals. You'll be surprised at the changes you'll see when they're developed."

Dutifully, Rusty snapped her first photo.

They sat in silence. Rusty realized once again how little experience she'd had making conversation with Daniel. They'd fought, or they'd discussed duties that needed to be taken care of, or they'd joked with each other. But at no time, except on the momentous night before Julia Rose's birth, had they tried to carry on a real conversation. Now she could think of nothing to say. "Are you finding it as hard to think of something to talk about as I am?" she asked finally.

"Most women could talk the leg off an iron pot," Daniel said. "I'm glad you don't."

She felt herself relaxing. She had always hated making useless conversation. "I'm glad I don't have to with you."

Minutes later she snapped another picture.

Daniel put his arm around her waist when she sat back down. "Are you getting cold?"

She wasn't, but she wanted his arm right where it was. "That feels good." She leaned her head against his shoulder.

"I reckon you're not the person I thought you were."

She suspected no greater compliment could have been tendered. "No?"

"No."

"I reckon you're not, either." She looked up at him and made a face. "I thought you were insensitive and arrogant and totally without any redeeming qualities."

"That bad?"

"At least that bad. Maybe worse."

"I thought you were stuck-up and prissy and too cute for your own good."

Rusty slipped her hand around Daniel's waist until they were closer still. "Every time you did something nice, I'd think, 'That's strange, I'd never have expected Daniel to act that way.' It didn't occur to me that I might have been mistaken about you all along. Maybe that's because you're so different from the men I know. But I think I like your differences. Most of them, anyway."

He smiled as though her words pleased him. "I thought you'd ruin this trip. I expected you'd hate it and yammer at me the whole time."

"Well, I did get lost and I did get sunburned after you warned me."

"And you did lie about knowing how to cook."

Rusty turned her face into Daniel's chest. "When did you figure that out?"

"After one meal. But like I've told you before, you crack hardy, I'll give you that. Getting the others to do the cooking was right brilliant. Straight out of your Mark Twain's *Tom Sawyer*, wasn't it?"

"I make a nice fettuccine."

Daniel threaded his fingers through her curls and tugged until she was looking at him. "No worries. It's you that's been important, not your cooking. I've never had a trip go so well. I've watched the way you make it all easy for the passengers. You're warm and funny and helpful. They love you."

She bit her lip. "But I lied."

"No one gave you much of a blooming chance to tell the truth." He touched her lip. "Stop biting that. I've got plans for it."

Kissing Daniel was beginning to seem absolutely natural. They had shared so many kinds in their short relationship: teasing kisses, passionate kisses, kisses meant to impress others. None had felt quite like this one, though. None had seemed exactly right, like two pieces of a jigsaw puzzle coming together.

"It's time for another picture." Daniel pulled away, but only far enough to search her eyes.

With a smile Rusty held the camera out to her side and snapped a picture without taking her eyes off Daniel's. "Done."

"You don't act like a tourist."

"I don't feel like a tourist. I feel like I'm home."

"At the Rock?"

"In Australia. At the Rock. With you."

"Strange talk for an American city girl." Their lips met again and again, joining in new ways, with new intensity. Daniel's arms circled her back, and he pulled her as close as he could. Still they strained to get closer. Rusty let her fingers slide through his hair. The air grew colder, the night darker. And finally, when Daniel moved away and turned her slightly, she saw that the Rock was a velvet-textured fireball.

Daniel's voice was husky. "It's different every time I see it. This is one of the best."

"I'm glad I'm seeing it with you."

"So am I."

Rusty knew that nothing would ever touch this memory—watching the Rock fade into the darkness with Daniel's arms around her.

They walked back to the Mog with a new understanding of each other. Rusty couldn't help but wonder where it would lead, and she couldn't help but wonder if now, sharing a tent with Daniel was going to be excruciatingly difficult.

At the campground they found most of the passengers sitting around the picnic table companionably looking through Peter's photographs. Someone had bought wine to share, and John was playing the harmonica. Everyone looked comfortable and very content.

"Peter, we ought to get you to snap this picture for the Outback Odysseys brochure." Rusty accepted a glass of wine and passed it to Daniel, accepting another one for herself. "We could call it A Peaceful Night in the Bush."

Suddenly Jill shrieked, slapping the table and destroying the atmosphere entirely. "I know where I've seen you!" She pointed to Rusty. "You sly dog!"

Everyone was silent, and all eyes were turned to Rusty.

Rusty was sure it would do no good to pretend that she was confused about what Jill was referring to. "Okay." She smiled. "My secret's out. No big deal."

"What secret?" Daniel rested his hand on Rusty's shoulder. "Don't tell me she's keeping secrets from me already."

"Surely Daniel knows." Jill's voice was more subdued.

"Daniel knows I was a model."

Jill's smile was relieved. "Good. I thought I was about to blow the cover-girl cover-up of the year."

"What's this all about?" Sally leaned forward and took the picture from Jill's hand. She squinted at it. "This is just a picture of Rusty coming out of the shower block at Wilpena."

"It was seeing her wet that made me realize who she was. Don't you have Aura shampoo here?"

Everyone's head-shaking was so rhythmic it was almost synchronized.

Jill laughed. "That's why you don't know what I'm talking about. Aura shampoo's a very popular brand in the States. And Rusty is the Aura Girl, only on the commercial she comes on and says, Jill lowered her voice, 'Hello, I'm Russet Ames...'" She stopped. "There's more, but I don't remember it."

"Neither do I." Rusty sipped her wine.

"You cut off all your glorious hair." Jill explained her statement to everyone else. "Rusty's hair used to be way down her back. Women all over the country wanted hair like that."

"That's because they didn't have to take care of it." Rusty forced herself to continue sounding casual. She had just noticed that Daniel's hand was no longer on her shoulder. She turned to see a peculiar expression on his face.

"I don't think I've ever heard of another model who made the kind of splash you did. And yet, here you are, cooking for us and married to Daniel." Jill shook her head. "Imagine that."

"Imagine that," Daniel echoed.

"Hey, I might even have some pictures of the Aura Girl. I've got a couple of American magazines with me that I haven't had time to look at." Jill stood. "Does anybody want to see?"

Everyone was as interested in this new development as Jill. Everyone except Daniel. "I've got some work to do," he said, turning back to the Mog. "Save the pictures for me if you find them."

Rusty watched him go. She had never lied about her modeling career, just as she'd never tried to draw attention to herself by bragging about it. She could not understand Daniel's sudden moodiness. What difference did any of it make? The passengers were excited, but no one was treating her any differently. She was still Rusty not Russet. She felt sure that once the excitement wore off, no one would give it a second thought unless it was to tease her from time to time.

Jill returned with the magazines, and there in the center of one of them was Russet Ames, the Aura girl, with her hair cascading over a plush white towel and her eyes with a come-hither sparkle. Rusty couldn't believe it was herself.

She shook her head. "Lord, I'm glad I'm not doing that anymore."

"Wasn't it exciting?" Amanda held the magazine and stared at the ad as if it had come from another world. Which it had, Rusty admitted to herself. New York and Outback Australia might be on the same planet, but just barely.

"It was exciting, but it wasn't very real. Does that make sense? I never wanted to be a model. My agent discovered me behind the counter of a department store when I was a college student. I never felt real, modeling. I feel real here."

Peter looked at the slick magazine photograph, and then he looked at the photograph of Rusty up against the ghost gum tree. "This one is the real you," he said, handing her his own handiwork. "The other one's just an image."

"I like your hair short better." Amanda closed the magazine with a decided snap. "And I like your freckles. I'd be afraid of you the other way."

"Seems to me a little fear wouldn't have done you any harm," Jill told the teenager, with a smile to soften her words.

Surprisingly, Amanda could laugh at the reference to her crush on Daniel. "Maybe so, but I'd rather have Rusty as a friend than some sort of an idol."

Rusty thought about Amanda's words as she got ready for bed later that night. As Daniel had predicted, the group had misplaced their tent, and she had been forced to search until she'd found it at the outskirts of the large camp-ground. Now, as she pulled on her nightgown and brushed her hair, she wondered if she could ever go back to the life she'd led before. She doubted it. But if she went back to New York and tried to get a different kind of job, she'd have to give up her expensive apartment. Her life-style, her friends—all of it would change.

Somehow that didn't matter. The apartment had never been much of a home, the friends who mattered would stay close no matter how many miles she put between them. If she was going to start over, it didn't have to be in New York. There was no real reason to go back there unless she returned to modeling. Her parents were retired, living in the Adirondacks as they'd always wanted to do. She had no other relatives except Alan and Penny. She was as free as a bird.

Except that a certain man had clipped her wings.

She didn't want to go back to New York. She wanted to stay here, or rather, she wanted to stay wherever Daniel was. The question wasn't really "What do I want to do with my life?" It was "Will I be able to do what I want?"

Russet Ames was in love with Daniel Marlin.

Rusty stared at her hairbrush and tried to figure out how such a preposterous thing had come to pass.

The rasp of the tent zipper startled her out of her reflections.

"So you're back." Daniel came in and left the tent flap open, closing the mosquito netting after him so that the campground lights could illuminate the inside of the tent.

"Where did you disappear to tonight, Daniel?" Rusty began to brush her hair again for something to do. She wished he'd waited until she'd had a chance to examine her feelings and put them in perspective. "I thought you'd be walking over to the Sheraton with the rest of us. They had a bush band playing in one of the lounges, and we all danced.''

"Good on ya." Daniel sat down on his sleeping bag and began to strip off his boots. "A little simple Aussie fun. Good for a city girl."

Rusty tried to ignore Daniel's patronizing tone. "I've always liked country music. This was a little different, but close enough to seem familiar."

"Now you can go home and tell everybody about it." Daniel pulled off his other boot.

"I'm in no hurry to go back." Rusty knew something was wrong, but she didn't know what. Apparently this had to do with the revelation of her success as a model. She decided to take a chance. She moved beside him, putting her hand on his knee. "Will you please tell me what's going on?"

"Don't get yourself in a flap."

"No worries, huh?" She moved her hand back to her own lap. "You know, I never lied to you about being successful as a model. I remember distinctly trying to get you to listen. But you thought so little of my attributes, you couldn't believe it."

"I believe it now." Daniel unbuckled his belt. "You can stay right there, but I do plan to take all these clothes off."

"Why should my success make a difference?"

Daniel unsnapped his pants. "No difference."

Rusty could feel her frustration build. "Then what is it? I'm still the same person you kissed tonight, Daniel. What you see is what I am."

He looked at her, but his eyes were disinterested. "Very nice, but then you've been told that often enough, haven't you?"

There was nothing else she could say that wouldn't be an admission of her feelings for him. She closed her fingers into fists, but she got up without another word and sat on her own sleeping bag. She turned away so he could undress in privacy. "I never thought you'd be the kind of man who couldn't stand a successful woman. Correction—I did think you were that kind of man at first, that kind of man and worse. I guess my first impression was the right one."

"Maybe."

"I'm proud of who I was."

"Good-o."

"You're the worst kind of male chauvinist. I'm glad I found it out now, before..." She stopped, acutely conscious of what she'd been about to say: Before I told you I loved you; before I made a complete idiot of myself.

"Before?"

She wondered if she'd imagined the interest in his voice. She turned to see him safely covered by his sleeping bag. She searched his eyes for the same interest she had heard in his voice, but they were carefully veiled. She sighed. "Before I get back to Adelaide. Now I can tell Penny I was right about you all along."

He grinned, but it was mechanical. There was no warmth in it. "Why don't I show you what a chauvinist I am?" He stretched the distance between them and grabbed her wrist. "I'll show you how a real Australian man communicates." He tugged her toward him. "Think of it as more educating; one more thing to learn before you go home."

"Let go of me, Daniel." Rusty tried to pull away, but his grasp was like steel. In a moment she was in his arms.

"We've been heading for this moment since the airport." Daniel's lips trailed down Rusty's cheek. "You threw your arms around me, and I wanted you like I've never wanted any woman."

Rusty stopped struggling, shocked by his words.

"And it's built and built until sometimes I think I'm going crazy. But that's all it is—physical. You want me, too. We can both get it out of our systems now." His lips found hers in a bruising kiss.

Rusty put her hands against Daniel's chest and pushed. "Stop it! I'm not really your wife and even if I were, you couldn't treat me like this!" She pushed again, but it did her no good.

"You don't have to act with me, Russet Ames. Don't you think I know what all that temper is about? You want me too, so you fight with me every chance you get to keep me away."

"I'm not acting. I don't want you when you're like this. What's wrong with you, Daniel? What have I done?"

He pulled her on top of him and locked his arms around her. "You came here and threw yourself into my life."

"I didn't. None of this was my choice. You know it wasn't!"

"I know you don't belong here. This is a lark, a holiday. In a few weeks you'll go back to New York and prance around in front of some camera half-naked again."

"You don't know anything about me!"

"I know you're a city girl. My mother was a city girl." Abruptly he let her go. Rusty slid down to his side but she didn't move any farther.

"Daniel, you're not making any sense. What is it? What's bothering you? Please tell me."

There was no answer.

"Please talk to me. How can I help, what can I do, if you don't talk to me?"

"Get in your sleeping bag."

"Not until you tell me what's wrong."

His arms came around her again. "I know an invitation when I hear one."

"Let go of me. I don't want you. Not like this." She wrenched away from him. "I don't want you at all. Not at all!"

"We both know that's not true." Daniel's eyes were gleaming, but he brushed a wrinkle out of his sleeping bag as if nothing had happened. "I guess you prefer city men as lovers—men who'll treat Miss Russet Ames like the piece of pretty china she is."

"I've never had a lover." Russet sat down on her sleeping bag and began to unzip it with unsteady fingers. "Not that it matters, does it? But you're so busy trying to believe the image of me as some highly paid floozy that you can't see I'm not that way at all."

"You expect me to believe that the woman sizzling on the pages of Jill's magazine is as pure as the shampoo she uses?"

"I don't expect you to believe anything."

"It wouldn't matter to me, anyway. You'll go back to New York and make another million or two. You won't even remember this trip." Daniel lay back with his hands under his head.

"I can promise you I'm going to try hard to forget it!"

Rusty zipped her sleeping bag closed and burrowed as far into it as she could go. She could hardly believe that the night that had held such promise had been shattered by Daniel's anger. What had she done except make a success of a career she'd never even wanted?

It was only days later when she realized Daniel's final words that night had provided the answer she was searching for—only she'd been too upset to really hear them.

"You'll forget the trip," he said heavily, "and you'll forget me and this night. You've got a life that none of this fits into and before long, even the memory of it will be gone like the glow of the Rock when night finally falls."

Chapter Eleven

November 8th

Dear Sly,
We visited a camel farm this afternoon. A camel just like the one on this card hissed and spat at me, then he tried to bite my foot. In spite of that, I rode him around the paddock. Every pound I've gained melted away when he decided to trot on the way back. I think it's time to come home to New York. The subways seem safe by comparison.

Peevishly,
Rusty

"I could get your pillow out of the back if you'd like."

Rusty narrowed her eyes at Daniel's little joke and lowered herself into her seat, trying not to grimace as her bottom made contact with it. "It's fine for you to laugh; I didn't see you riding one of those beasts."

"Oh, I never have. They don't look safe to me at all."
Daniel pulled the Uni-Mog out to the road and turned it
toward Alice Springs.

"And here I thought you probably owned a string of
camels and rode them through the Outback for days and
days looking for secret water holes or stray dingos or
whatever it is that you real Aussie men do." Rusty clamped
her lips together and turned her attention to the windshield in front of her. She was hot, and tired, and increasingly temperamental. The trip was no longer fun. It was
just something to be gotten through—like a final exam or
a tonsillectomy.

"The Outback was opened up by camel caravans, but
today camels are hardly more than feral pests."

"Save the lecture for the passengers, Daniel. I'm going
to close my eyes and see if I can get some sleep."

She badly needed sleep, but Rusty knew it wasn't going
to come. Not with the Mog swaying beneath her and Daniel sitting next to her. Daniel was the reason she needed
sleep, anyway.

It had been three days since the sunset at Ayers Rock.
That night might not ever have happened, judging by
Daniel's attitude toward her. He was back to treating her
like a not-too-bright kid sister. Now, of course, his jokes
centered around shampoo and modeling, but no one lis-
tening would think of them as anything other than the af-
fectionate humor of a husband toward his beloved wife. No
one but Rusty, that is.

Rusty heard the sarcasm and the insult in Daniel's words.
She was increasingly hurt by his attitude. She had done
nothing to him; she deserved none of what she was getting. Yet Daniel seemed to believe her guilty of something.

She had today to get through and part of tomorrow before Daniel took the passengers to the airport to catch their

flights home from Alice Springs. Perhaps then, on the drive back to Adelaide, she and Daniel would have the chance they needed to work through this sudden impasse in what once had been a blossoming relationship.

In the meantime, she had all she could do to swallow her irritation and count the minutes until the trip ended.

They stopped at a clearing not far from the roadside for lunch. By now, lunch preparations were second nature to her and as Daniel made a small fire to boil the billy, she got out sliced beef from the past night's dinner and a variety of salads, some canned and two fresh that she'd prepared the night before. The passengers were filing past the serving table in a matter of minutes.

Rusty pulled her camp stool to the fire with everybody else's and started eating.

"Am I imagining it, or has the tucker gotten better as the trip went on?" Jill winked at Rusty, but she addressed the question to Daniel.

"It got better when you passengers took over the cooking." Daniel answered.

Jill's eyes widened behind her wire-frame spectacles.

"Daniel knows you had to teach me what to do," Rusty explained. "What he doesn't know is that I've been doing the cooking myself for the past four nights. He conveniently forgot to notice that."

"And a good job you've done of it," Sally said, coming back with seconds on her plate. "You're an accomplished camp cook now."

Rusty tried to laugh. "Now, when I have dinner parties, I'll have to start a campfire in the kitchen. Otherwise I won't know what to do." She thought of the sterile business dinners she'd dutifully cooked fettuccine for, and this time, her laughter was real. "I've got a better idea. I'll take everybody down to Central Park and have a cookout there.

Then we can eat our damper and drink our billy tea at the local police station."

"You talk like you're going back to New York." Jill handed Perry a piece of cake from her plate. "Aren't you staying in Australia? Or is Daniel going back to the U.S. with you instead?"

Rusty didn't know what to say. After almost two weeks of pretending to be married to Daniel, she still slipped up from time to time.

"Visa problems," Daniel said finally. "Rusty's got to go back and reapply to enter the country as a permanent resident."

"What a shame. I don't know how the two of you'll stand being separated. Such a pair of lovebirds." Jill stood and went to wash her dishes.

Rusty couldn't look at Daniel. Lovebirds? Mad dogs would be more like it.

"We'd better push on." Daniel stood, too.

The trip to Alice Springs was subdued. There had been too much to eat and too many miles behind them. People read or chatted quietly, but there was none of the hilarity that had characterized the beginning of the tour. Everyone felt the ending that was coming—Rusty most of all.

Alice Springs appeared out of nowhere, ringed by the colorful MacDonnell Ranges. "The Alice," a town of 22,000 in the geographical center of the continent, lay like a tiny flower-bedecked oasis in the middle of miles and miles of red sand plains. The MacDonnell Ranges themselves offered enough beautiful gaps, gorges and chasms hidden within them to make the area a tourist mecca, but it was the town itself and its unique Outback spirit that many came to enjoy.

They camped at a small park just at the edge of town. No sooner had they put up their tents than Daniel rounded up the passengers again to take them to nearby Standley Chasm and Simpson Gap to admire the local scenery.

"I'll stay behind and work on dinner," Rusty told Daniel. "You go on without me."

Something flickered behind Daniel's eyes, and for a moment Rusty wondered if it might be disappointment. "It's a tradition to get takeaway chicken and chips here," he told her, his voice nonchalant. "You don't have to cook if you don't want to."

She would like to have believed that Daniel wanted her to come, but days of being either teased or ignored had taught her too well not to get her hopes up. "I'd hate to do that to everyone on our last night," she said, scuffing her sandal in the sand and watching the patterns it made. "Besides, you'll enjoy it more if I'm not along. You won't have to think of anything else to hassle me about."

He tipped his hat, his eyes colder than they'd been, and climbed into the Mog. In a moment he was gone.

Why had she challenged him that way? She wanted things to be better between them, and yet she was still suffering from the things he had said to her on their last night at Ayers Rock. As hard as she'd tried to fight it, she was still in love with the man, and obviously people in love did things they wouldn't normally do. She was proud and stubborn, but she wasn't a shrew. She did not want Daniel to remember her this way.

Since they were scheduled to go to the casino that night, Rusty decided to have dinner ready when everyone returned. She would fix it herself, and it would be a meal to remember. Bush tucker wouldn't do tonight. She counted out the money she had left from her food allotment. There was more than she'd hoped. Surprisingly, she'd done well on shopping and planning meals, if not so well at cooking them. She walked into town, admiring the brilliant lavender jacaranda trees dotting the landscape. The Alice was a blooming garden of pink and white oleander, scarlet bougainvillea, and purple morning glories.

She had never lived in a town this size—it seemed hardly more than a dot on the map—but as she strolled along, admiring the neat little shops and the well-kept streets, she realized there was nothing missing in Alice Springs that she couldn't live without. Residents wished her a good-afternoon and an aborigine girl carrying a smaller edition of herself flashed a fantastic smile that some of Rusty's model friends would have envied. The sun was warm, but the heat was dry and healing, and by the time Rusty arrived at the modern supermarket where she planned to do her shopping, she was beginning to put her problems in perspective.

In the taxi on the way back to the campground she planned an attack on Daniel's senses. The idea had come to her as she'd shopped. Somewhere between the coffee and the cereal she'd realized how foolish her anger was. She hadn't fallen out of love with Daniel. As hard as she'd tried to convince herself that she had, she hadn't been able to. He was still arrogant, infuriating Daniel Marlin, but under that was the deeply sensitive man who could handle anything except his own stubborn pride. And that was something that she of all people should understand.

Daniel cared about her. None of what he'd said to her made any sense at all unless he cared. She had to show him she was safe to fall in love with. She had waited twenty-four years to fall in love. She would wait as long as it took for Daniel to trust her.

She had been going about everything the wrong way. Now that she'd had some time to think, she realized just how whiny and petty she'd been in the past days. Her modeling success—or perhaps the money she'd made from it—had made him see her in a different light. She was no longer the Rusty he knew; instead she was Russet Ames, a commodity that belonged exclusively to a shampoo company in America. Daniel had to be taught that neither her success nor her money made any difference. His male ego had to be stroked. He had to see that she believed he was more important than anything else.

At the campsite she started a fire so she would have enough coals to grill the steaks she'd bought. The zucchini and corn on the cob would be cooked on the gas grill, but she wrapped potatoes in foil and placed them around the fire to be put into the coals when the fire burned down. She opened cans of mushrooms and put them in a saucepan to heat, and she sprinkled chives and bacon bits in two of four containers of sour cream.

By the time the Mog pulled up, everything was ready except the steaks. And by the time the passengers had washed up and gotten their plates and cutlery, the steaks were ready, too.

The meal was an outstanding success. Rusty basked in the compliments and watched with pleasure as everyone filled their plates to overflowing. Although Daniel said nothing, she noticed he went back for seconds, and that was praise enough.

She cleaned up with brisk efficiency and lots of help. John pulled out his harmonica, and Annette was persuaded to play her guitar. They drank tea and sang until the sky was dark above them. A magpie warbled in a nearby tree, continuing its song when theirs was finished.

"Let's go around the circle and say what we liked best about the tour," Rusty said, not wanting the group to break up too quickly.

"That's easy. Everything," Perry began. "I liked it all."

"I liked the feeling of getting off my camel alive," Jill said.

"I liked finding out I still had friends after I acted like such a case up on Ayers Rock." Everyone applauded Amanda's words.

They continued around until they came to Daniel. "Rescuing a certain redhead from a gum tree." He looked at Rusty but there was no characteristic grin. "That's something I'll never be able to forget."

"Having to search for my tent a couple of nights," Rusty said, last of all. "And, of course, sharing that tent with my new husband." They all applauded again. Rusty caught Daniel's gaze and held it. "You've all heard of tea and toast?" She held up her cup. "Well this is a tea toast. To all of you, the best lot of passengers ever. And to Daniel, a tour guide who made this trip memorable for each of us."

"And to Rusty," Peter said, "who cooked some of the most memorable meals any of us have ever had."

"And to Rusty," Daniel echoed, "the woman who made this trip memorable for me." He swung his cup toward her and then he finished his tea in one swallow and stood. "We'll be leaving for the casino in an hour. Anybody who plans to go should be in the Mog at eight o'clock."

Rusty felt a thrill of excitement. She had scored, both with the meal and the toast to Daniel. He hadn't looked at her that way in days. And his toast to her! He actually admitted she'd made the trip memorable for him.

She felt almost giddy with excitement and relief. Things were going to turn out all right after all. She had to be patient; she had to be understanding. But there was hope for Daniel. There was hope for them both.

Inside their tent she rummaged through her suitcase for the appropriate dress to wear. She'd only brought two on the tour, and now, examining them both, she decided on the more daring one. It was no designer creation, but the amber jersey knit was the color of her eyes, and it clung to the new, lusher curves of her body until there was little left to the imagination. She had brought it because it packed well, but now she decided she'd made a wise decision. With gold jewelry it would be perfect.

On the way out of the tent she ran into Daniel, who was just coming in. They stood together in the entrance, neither of them in any hurry to move.

Rusty restrained the urge to put her arms around Daniel's waist and take the hug she wanted so badly. "I was just going up to have a shower and get dressed."

"Then you're going?"

"Are you?"

"I have to."

"Then I'm going."

He reached up and brushed a curl off her forehead. "Why'd you fix that flash dinner tonight?"

She decided honesty would be in order. "To get your attention."

He smiled a little. "Didn't you think you had it?"

"I thought maybe you despised me."

His finger brushed her cheek. "Do you really believe that?"

"I don't know what to believe. Only I do know that I don't want the trip to end this way for us." Tentatively she put her hand on his shoulder. "Do you?"

He said neither yes nor no, but he leaned forward and brushed his lips across hers. His hand came around her waist, and he pulled her closer. Then he kissed her again until every nerve in her body was screaming for something more.

"Go get ready." Daniel's hand dropped from her waist. "It won't be long before we leave."

Rusty took more care dressing than she had in months. When she was finished with her hair and her makeup, it was Russet Ames who stared back at her from the bathroom mirror. It was a Russet who was certainly different, but it was the New York model nonetheless. Her skin wasn't the fragile milk-white it had been, but it glowed with health and vitality. The clusters of cherry-colored curls would never compete with the extravagant beauty of the mane she'd so impetuously ordered shorn, but it suited her better, emphasizing the delicate lines of her features and the slight tilt of her brows. She examined herself with the impartial eye of a professional and knew she had never been prettier.

Daniel seemed to have come to the same conclusion. He stood at the door of the Mog waiting for her, and the look on his face was testimony to his feelings. "Quite an eyeful."

"And look at you. You're gorgeous." She admired this new Daniel. In honor of the occasion he was even wearing a dark blue sport coat to match his pants.

"You told me that once before," he reminded her with an easy grin.

"Ah, but then I didn't know who you were. I'll never make that mistake again."

"Maybe we've both made a mistake or two."

"Maybe."

"Come on, you two, let's get a move on," a female voice shouted from the Mog. "I've gotta go make some big bickies."

"Luanne thinks she's going to make a fortune tonight," Daniel explained, holding out his hand to help Rusty aboard.

"To think I'd live to see the day you start translating Australian slang for me."

The ride to the casino was short. The Diamond Springs Hotel Casino had none of the glitz or glitter Rusty had expected, but it did have a small, enthusiastic crowd of gamblers playing slot machines, or "pokies," and traditional betting games such as blackjack and baccarat. In one room a crowd of men stood in a circle and took turns flipping two coins and betting on the outcome in a uniquely Australian game called Two Up. In another area a keno game was going on while more leisurely gamblers sipped drinks and waited for their numbers to light up on a screen.

"Is it always this low-key?" Rusty waited for Daniel, who had gallantly held the door open while the passengers trooped inside.

"It has been every time I've come. I imagine it gets wilder on weekends."

"I was expecting a mini-Las Vegas."

"Disappointed?"

Rusty wondered exactly what answer Daniel wanted. The look that had accompanied the question had been nothing less than penetrating.

"Of course not. I filmed a commercial in Las Vegas. It was interesting, but not my scene at all. This is charming and classy—just right. But I'm not much of a gambler, I'm afraid, so I'm no expert."

"Ever play the pokies?"

"I lost a dollar on the slot machines in Las Vegas. That was enough for me."

"Come on, big spender, I'll treat you to a go." Daniel put his arm around Rusty's shoulders and guided her to a vacant machine.

One dollar later she stopped. "That was it, Daniel. I'm one of the unluckiest people you'll ever meet."

"Let's go have a drink."

They hadn't moved three feet from the machine before Luanne took it over. The last thing Rusty heard as they left the room was the clanging of bells and Luanne's shouts of joy. She poked Daniel in the side when he laughed.

They sat in a corner near the keno game and sipped a beer apiece. Rusty searched for a neutral subject and grabbed at the first available one. "How do they play keno?" She picked up one of the keno cards at their table and stared at it. "What do all these numbers mean?"

"The numbers go from one to eighty. You pick as many as you want, up to fifteen of them, and you bet that of the twenty numbers they pick, some portion of your numbers will come up."

Rusty frowned. "I don't understand."

Daniel pulled a card out to show her. "Like this. You mark the numbers you want," he marked six at random, "and then you figure out how much you want to bet and how many games you want to play on that card, then you mark that down here." He showed her on his card. "I've bet a dollar that some of my numbers will come up."

"A whole dollar?"

He grinned. "Another big spender. If three or four of my numbers come up I get a small payoff, if five come up I get a bigger one, and if six come up I get somewhere over a thousand dollars." He dropped the card on the table. "There are more complicated ways to do it, but that's the easy way."

"Aren't you going to turn it in?"

Daniel shook his head. "I reckon I'll just sit here and watch everybody else go broke."

"Well, I'm going to fill one out." Rusty took a card and tapped her pencil as she examined it. "What's your birth date?" She translated it into numbers as he told her and marked each one on her card. "A Leo, I should have known." She marked three more numbers.

"What did you mark that time?"

"My birth date." She looked at him and then down at her card again. She marked three more numbers.

"And that time?"

"The date we met." Rusty reached over and covered Daniel's hand with her own. "It was my luckiest day." As she watched, he turned his hand palm up and threaded his fingers through hers.

"I think you'd better play that card. I have a feeling it's a winner." Daniel squeezed her hand and then removed his. "No, I'll play it for you. Stay here."

He arrived back at their table just as the screen was cleared for the next game. He handed her the card she'd marked. "Everything's been recorded. Now all you have to do is watch the screen and collect your money when all the numbers are up."

"That sounds easy."

It was surprisingly easy. Rusty watched and marked the numbers she'd guessed as the numbers appeared on the screen. When all were up, she stuck her tongue out at the card. "And to think I almost had it."

"Had what?" Daniel sipped his beer, but his eyes were dancing.

"Had them all. But I only got six." She looked at him. "Too bad, huh?"

"Too bad." He sipped some more. "By the way, did you consider that six numbers might give you a prize anyway?"

"That's right, I forgot. You said if I just got some of the numbers I got a payoff. Maybe you'll get your money back."

"Maybe. Why don't you go up and see?"

Rusty stood in line and handed her card to one of the casino staff. "Did I win anything?"

Daniel was still nonchalantly sipping his beer when she returned, eyes glazed. "A hundred dollars," she gasped.

"That's a right sweet little profit."

"You bet ten on the card, not a dollar. How did you know?"

He didn't smile, but his eyes were warm. "That card couldn't lose."

Rusty wanted to shout or sing or throw her arms around Daniel and kiss him until they were bounced from the casino for indecent behavior. The hundred dollars didn't mean anything, but Daniel's answer did. Things were going to work out; she knew it. She bent to give him a quick, exuberant kiss when an unfamiliar voice stopped her.

"Excuse me, but aren't you Russet Ames, the Aura Girl?"

Rusty straightened and turned around to find the source of the question. Unfortunately the source was an older woman surrounded by a crowd of half a dozen friends. Every one of them was staring at her in awe.

"Well, I used to be," she began.

"We knew it!" The woman's accent was distinctly American, and the voices of her friends were, too.

"You've cut your hair."

"You're prettier in person than on television."

"My niece dyed her hair to look like yours, but her mother made her dye it back." The babble was unbelievable, but Rusty had experienced this kind of adulation before. She smiled and nodded. The women meant no harm. Meeting a celebrity, even just one who sold shampoo, was probably a big event in their lives. Unlike some of her model friends who felt their private life should never be intruded upon, Rusty never grew angry at this kind of attention unless it turned vicious.

"Are you visiting Australia?" she asked, and listened politely to their answers. She answered questions and chatted with them until they finally realized how long they had kept her. She scribbled her name across keno cards for each one of them and waved as they left the casino.

When she turned back to her table, Daniel was gone.

The trip to the campground was silent. Everyone was tired, and no one had either lost enough money to complain about or won enough to brag about. Rusty had spent the last hour of their allotted time at the casino looking for Daniel. She had been unsuccessful. At ten o'clock she had stood by the door of the bus with the passengers and watched him walking down the road toward them.

He had been his usual charming self to the passengers, but to Rusty he had been merely civil. To her question about his absence, he had only responded that he'd needed some fresh air.

Rusty knew it was the reminder of her fame that had prompted his quick retreat. As she'd guessed, Daniel couldn't stand to know that she'd been successful before meeting him. He was exactly the male chauvinist she'd always believed him to be. Unless she groveled at his feet and apologized for everything she was and ever had been, Daniel would not let her into his life. Even then he might not, because even if she tried to make herself as ordinary as possible, she might be recognized as Russet Ames again. Obviously, Daniel couldn't handle any reminder of Russet Ames in his life.

In the darkness of their tent, they undressed for bed without a word. Rusty was safely under the cover of her sleeping bag before she spoke.

"I'm going to fly back with the passengers tomorrow. I think it would be best."

"Right-o."

"I'll probably leave Adelaide before you get the Mog back there. I'm going to fly home to New York as soon as I can."

Daniel was silent.

"You can tell Mrs. MacCready we got a divorce or an annulment or whatever you want to tell her. You can tell her it was all my fault. I don't care."

"It doesn't matter. I won't be staying with Odysseys."

Despite her anger, Rusty had to know what he'd be doing. How could she picture him in the days to come if she didn't even know where he was? "What are you going to do?"

"Go walkabout."

"Why, Daniel?"

She imagined he shrugged, because no verbal answer was forthcoming.

"You've been an education," she said finally. "The kind I always hoped I never had to have."

"You've been an education, Yank. The kind I always thought I didn't want."

"Well, your education's over. Tomorrow you'll be rid of me."

The silence deepened, and when Rusty's tears finally began to fall, she smothered the sounds with her pillow so that she wouldn't disturb it.

Chapter Twelve

November 13th

Dear Sly,
I'll be back in the Big Apple by the end of the week.
I'll give you a call when I've settled in. We can discuss
my future then.

Rusty

"Wusty, don' go." Danny threw himself at the woman he
now called his "Wusty," and held on to her knees.

Rusty knelt and put her arms around the little boy.
"Danny, your mum and dad have promised they'll bring
you over to visit me soon. And I'll send you letters. I
promise I will."

"Don' go."

"Come on, sport. I need help down at the depot. Leave
Rusty alone now." Alan held out his hand and firmly
pulled his son away. "I'll be back in time to get you to the

airport tonight," he told Rusty. "If you're still sure you want to go."

"I'm sure." Rusty watched as Alan picked Danny up and carried him down the stairs. She could still feel the imprint of the little boy's arms and smell the fragrance of soap and peppermint that always clung to him. Wistfully she returned to her packing.

"I wish you'd stay till Christmas. You've never had an Aussie Christmas, Rusty. You owe it to yourself." Penny came into the room holding Julia Rose over her shoulder. She patted the baby's back as she watched Rusty fold clothes and place them neatly in her suitcase.

"I'd like to, I really would. But I have to get back and decide what I'm going to do with the rest of my life." Rusty came to the dress she'd worn four nights before at the Diamond Springs Casino and quickly slipped it under a pile. The silky jersey slithered across her fingers with a disturbing sensuality, and silently she vowed to give it to Goodwill when she got back to New York.

"Do you need to talk?" Penny sat on a chair next to the bed and rocked back and forth to keep the baby from fussing.

Rusty knew how worried Penny must be. Personal privacy was important to Penny, and she would never pry or even volunteer to help unless she believed it was essential. "Not really. It's very clear to me what I have to do, and that's get away from Adelaide before Daniel comes back."

"Then it is Daniel you're running away from."

"That wouldn't be my choice of words."

The doorbell interrupted Penny's next sentence. She stood, switching Julia Rose to her other shoulder. "I wonder who that could be? Maybe Alan forgot something. I'll just go have a look."

Rusty continued her packing. She knew she was being hopelessly sentimental, but each item seemed to hold some reminder of Daniel. The clothes she'd worn on the tour, the souvenirs she'd purchased, the photographs she'd taken. She came to the keno card that had seemed like such a good omen for her relationship with him. Slowly she tore it in two and dropped the pieces in the wastebasket beside the bed.

Penny knocked and came in before Rusty could answer. Her eyes were wide. She didn't even seem to notice that Julia Rose was crying. "It's Mrs. MacCready. And she wants to see you."

"I was going to let Daniel handle that one." Rusty slammed the suitcase shut, narrowly missing a fingertip. "It's just like him to leave me with the dirty work."

"I've never known Daniel to ask anyone to shoulder his burdens."

"Well, now I'm stuck with explaining everything to the Iron Maiden by myself." Rusty straightened her skirt. "Hey, whose side are you on, anyway?"

"Daniel's."

"You don't even know what happened!"

"I know enough, I think." Penny jostled the baby, but her next words were still punctuated by Julia Rose's screams. "I know you flew home when you could have driven with Daniel. I know you missed the best chance you'd ever have to learn who he really is."

"I know who he really is. He's a hopeless male chauvinist who's so threatened by the fact that I'm a person in my own right, he can hardly see straight!" Rusty knew she was shouting to be heard, but she didn't care. It felt good to yell at somebody, even if that somebody was Penny.

"Rusty, you've wallowed in your prejudices about Australian men ever since you got here. Just because Daniel's style is a little different from what you're used to, you've interpreted everything through some foolish stereotype you have. Men like Daniel have trouble expressing their feelings, so they joke or fight or say nothing.''

''Oh, Daniel's great at saying nothing!''

''Daniel was raised not to show emotions, but that doesn't mean he doesn't have them. And he's not a male chauvinist. He grew up in a world where men had one role and women another, and they had to live that way to survive. But he saw his own mother die from the life she was forced to lead. He'd never begrudge you a better life than she had.''

Rusty sat down on the bed. ''What are you talking about?''

''Daniel watched his mother die from backbreaking hard work and from raising child after child because her husband felt that was the way it should be. She was a city girl, like you, and she wasn't strong enough for what she had to face. Daniel left home as soon as he could get away. He'd never admit it, but he's never gotten over what happened to his mother. If you think he was upset because you're a person in your own right, it's only because you didn't look closely enough. And that's your problem, Rusty Ames, not Daniel's! Be quiet, Julia Rose!'' Penny turned on her heel and marched out of the bedroom.

Rusty stared after Penny. Was this the same, sweet woman who never had a bad word to say to anyone? It seemed Rusty was continually underestimating her. Before she could recover, Penny came back to stand in the doorway.

''One more thing. You have a guest downstairs, and whether you like it or not, you're going to have to handle her questions. Daniel isn't here.''

''Was everything you said true?''

"Every blooming word."

"Oh, Penny, I wish I knew what to think." Rusty shut her eyes for a moment. "If it were me, I could change. But I can't change Daniel. He won't even talk to me about what's important. He's never told me about his mother or even admitted he has feelings for me."

"Daniel would feel terribly foolish crying on your shoulder or telling you he loves you. It's not Daniel's style. You'll have to teach him to talk to you, and you'll have to teach him to say he loves you. But while you're teaching him, you might want to notice all the ways he shows you and remember that actions speak louder than words."

Rusty stood and straightened her skirt again. "It's too much of a risk. You're saying this because you want Daniel and me to be together." She tried to smile. "Even though nobody would figure out why if they'd heard you yelling at me."

"There are no risks except the biggest one—which is losing Daniel. And I wasn't yelling; I was merely speaking loudly enough to be heard over the baby." Penny managed a smile, too. "Do you want me to go downstairs with you?"

Rusty shook her head. "No, I have to do this without you. I don't want Mrs. MacCready to be angry at you as well as at me. It might affect Alan's job."

Rusty trudged down the stairs, gearing herself for battle when all she really wanted was to find a place to have a good cry. She hadn't told Penny or Alan about Daniel's plan to leave Outback Odysseys, and she wasn't going to tell Jane MacCready, either. If Daniel changed his mind, Rusty still wanted him to have his job waiting for him. But she had also decided she wasn't going to lie anymore. Lies had gotten her into this situation, and more lies weren't going to help. If she had to tell Mrs. MacCready the whole truth, she would. She could only hope that somehow she could make it all right for Daniel.

"Hello, Mrs. MacCready." Rusty walked through the living room and seated herself on a chair opposite the older woman's. A breeze played through the open windows, but Rusty noticed only the stifling heat and the nervous dampness of her palms.

"Hello, Miss Ames."

"May I get you something to drink? Tea? Coffee?" As she asked the polite questions, Rusty suddenly realized what Mrs. MacCready had called her. Miss Ames, not Mrs. Marlin. Had it been a slip of the tongue or did she know the truth?

"Nothing, thank you. I'm here strictly to talk."

Rusty examined the Iron Maiden. There was something different about her. The Iron Maiden wasn't an iron maiden anymore. Mrs. MacCready was wearing a rose blouse with a rose-and-blue flowered skirt, and she was wearing a touch of color on her lips and cheeks. She looked years younger. In fact, she was a very attractive woman.

"You look nice today," Rusty said sincerely. "Those colors suit you well."

The color in Mrs. MacCready's cheeks seemed to deepen. "Thank you. I wanted to talk to Daniel, but since he's not back yet, I want to leave my message with you. I'll speak to Alan later, and he can give Daniel all the financial details, but I thought you'd like to be the one to give him my news."

Rusty waited to hear that Daniel had been fired.

Mrs. MacCready pulled a sheaf of papers from her handbag. "My husband and I are putting Outback Odysseys up for sale. We're making the terms suitable so that Alan and Daniel can purchase the company. We'll sell the buses separately to one of the larger tour companies, but the two Uni-Mogs and all the Jeeps, as well as all the camping equipment and the company name and logo will go to Alan and Daniel. The leases on the depots here and in Alice will be transferred to them, and they can decide if they want to keep them or find something smaller until they're ready to expand."

Rusty just stared at her.

Mrs. MacCready set the papers on an end table. "Do you think Daniel will be pleased? I know Alan will be."

Rusty attempted to recover. Surprisingly her voice still worked. "Pleased? He'll be ecstatic. But why are you doing this? What are you going to do?"

Mrs. MacCready smiled, and Rusty realized she was seeing someone she hadn't known existed. "I'm going to Norfolk Island to live with my husband. We're buying a small hotel there. We're already well-fixed financially, and we don't need a huge amount of cash from the sale of the business. Doing it this way will provide us with a nice, steady income, and it will give Daniel and Alan a chance. Bill and I are fond of both of them."

Rusty could only guess the details of the reunion between the MacCreadys. But she could certainly see the results of it just by looking at the contentment on Mrs. MacCready's face. "This is such good news. Alan and Daniel will be thrilled."

"When do you expect Daniel back?"

"I...I don't know exactly."

"A good wife should always know where her husband is," Mrs. MacCready said, a ghost of a smile in her gray eyes.

Rusty felt miserable. How could she lie anymore? On the other hand, how could she tell the truth? If she did, she might ruin Alan and Daniel's chance to buy Odysseys. "I guess I'm not a very good wife," she said, examining the carpet.

"I guess you're not a wife at all, are you, dear?"

Rusty looked up, aware that her eyes were moist. She shook her head sadly.

"Oh, my dear, we all pushed you into that, didn't we?" Mrs. MacCready's voice was remorseful. "I'm so sorry."

Rusty didn't know what to say.

"I know you didn't get married. In fact I knew you weren't really engaged. I pushed you at Daniel like the old romantic fool I am." Mrs. MacCready stood, hands clasped behind her back, and walked to the window. "I thought I'd lost my own husband, and then you and Daniel came along pretending you were engaged so he could keep his job. It was as plain as the nose on your face you were both lying. But I saw the way he looked at you when you weren't watching, and I saw the way he kissed you, and I thought, 'That's a match made in heaven.'"

She paused and turned back to Rusty. "Isn't that ridiculous? I decided then that I'd force you into going on the trip with Daniel. I thought romance would blossom if you were together day in and day out like that. It all came together so perfectly. I knew Amanda was head over heels for Daniel, so I sent her along to get him out of her system. I knew if she was along you'd have to keep up the pretense. I guess I thought if my own romance was dying, at least I could get some pleasure knowing that I had helped start one for someone else."

"Oh, Mrs. MacCready." Rusty stood. She knew she'd been the victim of manipulation, but she couldn't feel anything except sympathy for the woman in front of her. "Please don't worry. They were the best two weeks of my life."

"You love Daniel, don't you?"

Rusty nodded miserably. "I do, but I threaten his ego or something. He'll never let himself love me."

Mrs. MacCready shook her head. "That doesn't sound like Daniel at all. Daniel's just like my Bill, a real Outback man. I guess that's why I'm so fond of Daniel and why he irritates me so much at the same time. Both he and Bill are always joking. You have to guess what either of them is feeling. They never learned how to express themselves. I thought Bill didn't love me anymore; that he went to Norfolk Island because all my criticisms and complaints about the company had finally driven him away. But that wasn't it. He went because he wanted me to have a chance to run Odysseys myself. Away from me, Bill began to understand that all my complaints were just ways to get his attention and be part of his life. And with Bill away, I realized how petty I'd been. When I did realize it and went to tell him, he was waiting for me."

Rusty realized Mrs. MacCready wasn't the only sentimental fool in the room. Her own eyes were filling with tears. "I'm glad for you. But Daniel's not waiting for me."

"Maybe he doesn't feel he can. Maybe he doesn't feel he has anything to offer you."

"What do I need, except him?"

Mrs. MacCready shrugged. "Did you ever tell him that?"

Alice Springs looked just the same as it had four days before. The sun was setting behind the MacDonnell Ranges, and the town was bathed in a rosy glow. Rusty was glad that she and Daniel would have their confrontation here.

She had been spurred to come by Penny's revelations and Mrs. MacCready's pleas. But it had been her recollection of Daniel's words on their last night at Ayers Rock that had sent her to the telephone to change her flight. "Soon the memory of this trip will be gone like the glow of the Rock when night finally falls," he'd said with uncharacteristic poetry.

Daniel believed she would forget the trip and forget him once she was settled in New York. He didn't believe or understand her willingness to give up the life she'd once known to stay with him in Australia. Daniel was afraid her feelings were fleeting, easily wiped away by the excitement of the city. And perhaps, after what he'd seen his mother go through, he believed that was best for her anyway.

The airport taxi pulled up in front of the ramshackle depot where Outback Odysseys serviced and stored some of their vehicles between trips. Rusty paid the taxi driver and stepped onto the dirt path leading up to the front door. "Could you wait, please?" she asked. "I may need you to take me somewhere else in a moment."

She had no idea if Daniel would be at the depot or not, but as she was walking up the path she heard a string of curses echoing from behind the closed doors. The slow, broad tones belonged to Daniel. She waved the taxi driver away.

The door was unlocked, but then why would Daniel have to bother with locks and keys in a place like Alice Springs? She opened it and walked inside, waiting a moment until her eyes adjusted to the darkness and her nose to the smell of oil and the tickle of dust. Daniel was nowhere in sight. But there were two legs sticking out from under a Uni-Mog. Both the moleskin-clad legs and the Mog were familiar.

Rusty tiptoed over to stand nearby. "Do you need me to hand you some tools?" she asked softly.

There was a long silence and no perceptible movement under the Mog. Then, "Who said I needed anything?"

"I thought maybe you might need some help even if you didn't ask." I thought maybe you might need me, she added silently.

"I reckon I've managed right well without anybody's help."

"I reckon you have."

There was a loud clatter under the Mog and a cleaned-up version of the curses she'd heard when she'd been coming up the walk. "There's a wrench right there by my foot," Daniel said. "Slide it under here, would you?"

Rusty did as she'd been asked, kneeling by Daniel's feet. "Is that the one?"

"Right-o."

Rusty waited until the clatter died down again. "Why are you here so late?"

"Why are you here at all?"

"I brought you some news."

Daniel was suddenly still under the Mog. "What kind of news?"

"The MacCreadys want to sell Outback Odysseys to you and Alan. The terms are perfect. Alan says you can manage the payments and still make some of the innovations you want to."

There was no exclamation of joy from under the Mog. "Alan could have called me."

Rusty felt completely deflated. Whose idea was this, anyway? Had she really been crazy enough to think that Penny and Mrs. MacCready might be right? Had she really twisted Daniel's enigmatic statement until it had become a poem to unrequited love? She was no different from anyone else. If she wanted to believe something badly enough, she did, whether it made sense or not. She was a complete idiot.

She stood and headed for the door. It slammed loudly behind her. The cab was gone, and the center of town was more than a mile away. But it wasn't too far for someone with as many tears to walk off as she had. Rusty started down the road. She'd spend the night at one of the hotels she'd seen and head back to Adelaide in the morning. Blinking rapidly she increased her pace.

"Look around you, Yank!"

Rusty kept walking, but she slowed down a little to let Daniel catch up with her.

"Just what do you see here? Nightclubs, discos, gourmet restaurants? Boutiques? You can buy souvenirs in Alice, but just try to buy a designer dress."

Rusty kept walking, refusing to look at him.

"There's nobody in Alice Springs to take pictures of a pretty girl and sell them for millions."

"So what?" Rusty sniffed.

"I'll be living here when I'm not on trips. I'll stay here, Alan will stay in Adelaide. We'll run the company from both ends, the way we always planned."

"So what?"

"So this!" Daniel gripped her arm and forced her to stop. "There's nothing for you here. Can you see that? Can you see me? Look at me, blast you! Don't you think I'd change who I am for you if I could? But I can't change. I'm me, Daniel Marlin. I can't fit into your world. There's no place for me there. And I reckon there's no place for you here."

Rusty did look at him. She saw the man she loved, brown-haired, broad-shouldered Daniel Marlin with no smile on his handsome face and no light in his beautiful eyes. Her own eyes began to flash with anger.

"There's nothing wrong with Alice Springs. You're just using that as an excuse. What you mean is there's no place here for someone who's already made her mark on the world!" Rusty jerked her arm from his grasp. "You can't stand the fact that I was somebody, can you? It hurts your stupid pride! You're afraid I'll lord it over you or make you feel small because I have more money than you do, or..."

Daniel shook his head slowly. "You're as barmy as a bandicoot! I don't care about that."

"Then what do you care about? Do you care about me at all? Do you? Nod your head if you can't make yourself say it, Daniel. I have to know."

He stood silent and still.

Rusty turned and began to walk away.

"I care."

The words were so soft, that at first she wondered if she'd heard them. Rusty faced him again. "Did you say what I think you said?"

His nod was almost imperceptible.

"Then, if you do care, why can't we work something out? Don't you know by now that I love you? I'll be anything to you I can possibly be. I'll marry you, sleep with you, bear your children, scrub your floors, cook your meals..."

"Let's not get carried away." He smiled a little.

"Well, maybe you'll have to cook, unless it's outdoors." She couldn't smile back because her lower lip was trembling. "I'll fit myself into your life here, Daniel. That's all I want. I want to make my life with you."

"Listen to you. Do you think I'd ask for any of that? I know who you are, and I know who you've been. I saw the way you spoke to those women at the casino. You loved it. Stay here a few years and nobody will ever recognize you again. No, it'd be a fair cow to expect you to change for me. My mother tried to do that for my father, and it killed her."

Rusty looked down at the dress she'd purposely chosen for this meeting. It was the most expensive one she'd brought to Australia with her. She'd done her hair and makeup as if she were going on a modeling assignment, and her heels were high enough to almost bring the top of her head to Daniel's eye level. Every inch of her was Russet Ames.

"Look at me," she said, smoothing the violet silk skirt. "This is me, Daniel. I like this me, and I always will."

"I like it, too."

"But even when I was modeling, I wasn't happy being this way all the time. Sometimes I'd put my hair up under a baseball cap that belonged to a teenager down the hall, and I'd put on cutoffs and an old T-shirt and run around Central Park turning cartwheels and doing handstands. That was me, too." She paused. "The me that never was was the girl in all those commercials. I got sucked into modeling. Have you forgotten I got out of it before I ever met you? I cut my hair. I left New York. And I don't want to go back, not really."

"You can say that now."

She shook her head. "I can say it now, knowing I can say it in ten months or ten years, too. I'm not your mother, Daniel, and Alice isn't some isolated cattle station. You're not asking me for anything I don't want to give. You never would. You never could."

"I'm not asking you for anything."

"But you want to, don't you? I've gone as far as I can go. You have to do the asking now. Just know that I'll say yes, whatever you ask, because I know I can trust you."

Daniel crossed his arms across his chest. "It's hot here in the summer, hotter than anything you've ever seen. Do you know that people in Alice entertain themselves by having boat races in the Todd River, only there's no water, so they have to cut holes in the boats and run instead?"

Rusty smiled even though her lip was still trembling. "I'd like to see that."

"And the insects get worse, not better."

"I can handle heat and insects, and I can handle boat races in a dry riverbed. I can handle the peace and quiet and friendly people and the view of the MacDonnells and the feeling that I'm part of something unique and wonderful. What I can't handle is losing you." Rusty held out her hand.

Daniel just looked at it. "What about the man in New York? The one you write all those bloody cards to?"

"He's my agent and friend, for Pete's sake. Sly's fifty-seven and a grandfather."

"I'm just the man you know. I'm not some rough-cut diamond waiting for you to polish me."

"And I'm not the piece of pretty china you accused me of being once. You're arrogant and opinionated and sometimes your Outback ways drive me to distraction, but Daniel, I love you anyway."

"And you're stubborn and proud and everything I always stayed away from, Yank." He held out his hand, but it was still inches from touching hers. "If you take my hand now, you'd better know I'm not ever going to let go."

She was in his arms instantly. The night air turned cold around them, but still they kissed until neither had the breath to continue. "Daniel," Rusty said finally, "what does this mean exactly?"

"We'll get married." He kissed her again. "As fast as possible, because whatever patience I had is gone. The kids can wait a year or two, can't they? In the meantime, come with me on my trips. Let me show you the Kimberleys and the Gulf country, Cape York. All of it."

"About the floors..."

He squeezed her tight. "I know that was just so much yabbering."

"I want to be your partner, Daniel. In every way. In the company, in your life."

His smile was answer enough.

"And will you let me love you?"

He took her face between his hands and turned it to his. "Only as long as I can love you. Just forever."

She knew then that everything was going to be all right. She wouldn't hear those words often, but when she did, they would be even more special. "I guess that will do for a start."

"I guess it had better, Yank."

He kissed her hard. Then, hand in hand, they walked through the streets of the town that would shelter them in all the days to come.

Epilogue

Annie, get Henry Biddler on the phone." Sly Jackson chomped on the end of one of the big cigars that he usually didn't pull out unless he had someone in the office to impress.

"You might want to read your mail first." Annie dropped a clump of letters on Sly's desk. "There's one from Miss Ames. Priority mail." With calm efficiency, Annie put Rusty's letter on the top before she left the room.

"About time! Henry's been getting impatient, and so have I!" Sly pulled the letter out of the envelope that Annie had neatly slit for him. The words seemed to jump off the page.

November 16th

Dear Sly,
You'll probably find this confusing, but this is a wedding invitation. My other marriage is off, but don't feel

badly. This one is to the same man. If you want more details, please book a flight out on the next plane because we're getting married next weekend. I promise your hotel will be first-rate and the bride will be beautiful.

Love and kisses,
Rusty

P.S. If you're wondering what to get me for a wedding present, a dozen bagels and a year's supply of lox would be perfect.

"Annie!"

"Yes, Mr. Jackson."

"Cancel the call to Henry, and call my analyst," he bellowed.

Sly's cigar landed on the floor in front of him, but he paid no attention because he never lit it anyway. "No, don't call Dr. Matson. Book me the next flight to," he picked up Rusty's letter and read the address, "to Alice Springs."

"Alice Springs, sir?"

"Australia. Alice Springs, Australia."

"Yes, sir."

Sly stared at the envelope for a full minute. "Annie," he shouted once more.

Annie came back to stand in the doorway. "Yes, sir?"

"What do you know about Australia, Annie?"

"Just the usual—you know, boomerangs and kangaroos. That sort of thing."

"How does this sound to you?" Sly held his hand up in front of him and swept it slowly in a line as he talked. "The scene opens with a horse riding across the plains. There are kangaroos hopping in front of him, and birds flying around, maybe a windmill or two somewhere, you know, typical Australia.''

"Yes, sir.''

"The horse gets nearer and we see a woman riding it. They come closer and closer, her hair bouncing in rhythm to the pounding of the horse's hooves. The girl springs off the horse and she's holding a bottle of shampoo in her hand. She says: 'Hello, I'm Russet Ames. Out here in the Outback we need all the conditioning we can get. Nothing does the job like Aura....'''

"Mr. Jackson?''

Sly shook his head as if to bring himself back to reality. "Yes, Annie?''

"That's probably the worst idea I've ever heard.'' Annie turned to go back in her office.

"Annie?''

"Yes, sir?''

Sly stood and held out his hand. "I think you just earned a raise.''

Annie shook it. "Thank you, sir. Anything else?''

Sly smiled. "Yeah. Just one more thing. When I'm safely on the plane, I want you to send a telegram to Henry. Make it simple. Something like, 'Russet Ames no longer considering new Aura contract. I've gone to Australia to relax, for a change. Suggest you go somewhere and do the same.'''

* * * * *

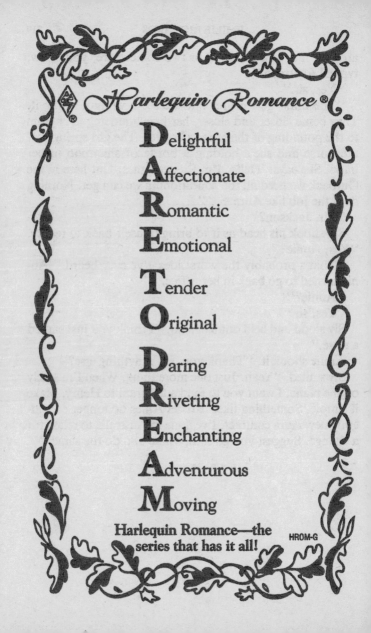

HARLEQUIN PRESENTS®

HARLEQUIN PRESENTS
men you won't be able to resist falling in love with...

HARLEQUIN PRESENTS
women who have feelings just like your own...

HARLEQUIN PRESENTS
powerful passion in exotic international settings...

HARLEQUIN PRESENTS
intense, dramatic stories that will keep you turning
to the very last page...

HARLEQUIN PRESENTS
The world's bestselling romance series!

Harlequin® Historical

If you're a serious fan of historical romance,
then you're in luck!

Harlequin Historicals brings you
stories by bestselling authors, rising new stars
and talented first-timers.

Ruth Langan & Theresa Michaels
Mary McBride & Cheryl St. John
Margaret Moore & Merline Lovelace
Julie Tetel & Nina Beaumont
Susan Amarillas & Ana Seymour
Deborah Simmons & Linda Castle
Cassandra Austin & Emily French
Miranda Jarrett & Suzanne Barclay
DeLoras Scott & Laurie Grant...

You'll never run out of favorites.

Harlequin Historicals...they're too good to miss!

HH-GEN

HARLEQUIN®

I N T R I G U E ®

THAT'S INTRIGUE—DYNAMIC ROMANCE AT ITS BEST!

Harlequin Intrigue is now bringing you more—more men and mystery, more desire and danger. If you've been looking for thrilling tales of contemporary passion and sensuous love stories with taut, edge-of-the-seat suspense—then you'll *love* Harlequin Intrigue!

Every month, you'll meet four new heroes who are guaranteed to make your spine tingle and your pulse pound. With them you'll enter into the exciting world of Harlequin Intrigue—where your life is on the line and so is your heart!

Harlequin Intrigue—we'll leave you breathless!

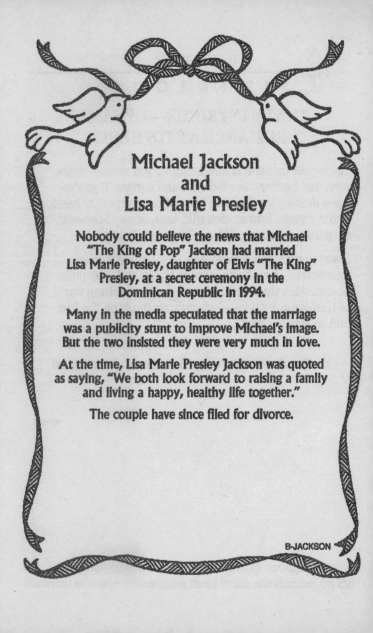

Michael Jackson
and
Lisa Marie Presley

Nobody could believe the news that Michael "The King of Pop" Jackson had married Lisa Marie Presley, daughter of Elvis "The King" Presley, at a secret ceremony in the Dominican Republic in 1994.

Many in the media speculated that the marriage was a publicity stunt to improve Michael's image. But the two insisted they were very much in love.

At the time, Lisa Marie Presley Jackson was quoted as saying, "We both look forward to raising a family and living a happy, healthy life together."

The couple have since filed for divorce.

B-JACKSON